The white [illegible] the angle of the house. Fuming with rage, [illegible] the front door and made my way to the withdrawing room. Since she had left school, Davinia had become even more rude, callous, bossy and selfish. It was impossible to see the attraction she had for any of the young men she had now started collecting.

A revving noise took me to the French windows. At the rear of the house was a small copse encircled by a gravel road that formed a natural racing track. The Jaguar was going round and round the circuit, braking at the bends and accelerating down the straits. The strange thing was that St John now seemed to be alone in the car. As each lap was completed, he was getting more and more excited and his face was one huge smile of delight. Then he suddenly rose in his seat and pressed the horn in a long, loud act of celebration.

The white Jaguar then limped to a halt. Davinia sat up beside him and I realized what must have happened. She had fallen asleep across him and he had used his horn to rouse her.

CHRISTOPHER T MOUNTJOY

Coming of Age
The Mountjoy Memoirs I

Futura

A Futura Book

This edition published in 1985
by Futura Publications, a Division of
Macdonald & Co (Publishers) Ltd
London & Sydney

ISBN 0 7088 2874 4

Typeset in Times by Fleet Graphics, Enfield, Middlesex

Printed and bound in Great Britain by
Hazell, Watson & Viney Ltd
Aylesbury, Bucks

Futura Publications
A Division of
Macdonald & Co (Publishers) Ltd
Maxwell House
74 Worship Street
London EC2A 2EN

A BPCC plc company

Chapter One: FAMILY MATTERS

I was born Christopher Titus Mountjoy, the third, last and luckiest child of two people who were, by any stretch of the imagination, fairly bizarre parents. Historical record has it that I came into the world one bright May morning at the family seat of Mountjoy Manor and that the event was so traumatic and exhausting for my dear mother that she did not have breath enough left to call for her customary gin and tonic. Since I was a breech delivery, I first presented my own version of the family seat and the physicians in attendance were thus able to determine my sex before they could assess any facial resemblance to my parents. In view of the life I was to lead, this accident of nature has taken on a special significance.

From the first, I was putting my best foot forward.

Feeling, as he did, that he had more than adequately discharged his paternal duty by making a brief appearance at my conception, my father was not there to witness my arrival. A week or so later, I understand, he got one of his secretaries to send a greetings telegram and in due course considerately arranged for another of his minions to represent him at the christening. On my first birthday, as a gesture of goodwill, he sent me a signed photograph of himself presiding at a board meeting. I like to think that it was father's way of expressing affection.

Though the front of heaven was not full of fiery shapes at my nativity and though the frame and huge foundation of the earth did not exactly shake like a coward, I realized instinctively that I was not in the role of common men. I was a Mountjoy. Set apart from mere mortals. Belonging to a higher order of reality. Not to put too fine a point on it, I had star quality.

It has proved to be at once a curse and a blessing.

Like so many illustrious English families, we come of French stock. The first of our line to settle here did so in 1310 and he quickly established a reputation as a courageous soldier and a shrewd horse dealer. His fame was to be short-lived. On 24 June 1314, he perished at Bannockburn while leading an unsupported charge against Robert Bruce, believing – erroneously as it turned out – that valour is the better part of discretion and that men who fight in tartan skirts are not to be taken seriously.

The bravery of Guillaume de Mountjoy did not go unrewarded. In recognition of the doomed solo assault on the heathen Scots, his son was granted a baronetcy and the estates in Herefordshire where the ancestral home stands to this day. A dynasty had been founded.

The Mountjoy family. Soldiers, statesmen, diplomats, travellers, judges, counsellors, heroes and whoremasters. Bold and enterprising characters whose proud steps have echoed down the corridors of history.

We have rubbed shoulders with royalty and taken it from there.

Above all else, the Mountjoys have shown a healthy pragmatism. This is nowhere seen more clearly than in the varying interpretations placed upon our family motto – NON SEQUITUR. For the Bannockburn Mountjoy, who led where nobody followed, it was an all too accurate epitaph but each of his successors has translated the words afresh to match his individual taste and circumstances. Three examples must suffice of this ability to breathe new life into dead Latin.

For my great-grandfather, Sir Edwin Mountjoy, a man whose mind moved at such a lethargic pace that he was in a state of permanent bewilderment, the revered motto meant simply 'I don't get it . . . '

For my grandfather, Sir Sholto Mountjoy, an inveterate

gambler who rode a streak of bad luck at cards throughout his life and who is best described as a latter-day Horatius at the bridge table, it always came out as a plaintive 'I can't follow suit . . . '

And for my father, Sir Marcus Mountjoy, a frank, fearless and forthright type who will make a decision and stand by it whatever happens, two words from an ancient language have become a defiant 'Damn the consequences!'

One family motto: three variations.

My whole life has been a search for a personal interpretation, for a phrase that will accommodate all the strange and wonderful experiences that have befallen me. I now invite you to accompany me on that quest.

NON SEQUITUR.

Please follow . . .

Mountjoy Manor stands at the heart of rural Herefordshire near the village of Hampton Magna. Like most things associated with my family, it is quite unique. It is less a home than a joyous compendium of architectural styles over a period of some six hundred years and it really has to be seen to be disbelieved.

What began as a fortified manor house suffered Middle Ages spread to become a rambling Tudor dwelling before being corseted by late Elizabethan symmetry. Further whalebone was provided by Stuart severity but a Baroque explosion then burst the stays completely. In an attempt to hold everything decently in place again, Georgian elegance supplied a white marble bodice but Regency extravagance loosened its buttons at once and added a spectacular Indian dome by way of a hat. Gothic extravagance brought garish colours and outlandish fashions, then Edwardian compromise tried to cover its shame with more simple garments. And so it has gone on.

Yet if the exterior is a triumph of incongruity, the interior is a model of uniformity. Rooms are vast, ceilings are vaulted, floors are paved and oak doors swing on massive iron hinges. But for the furniture and fittings, you might imagine the house to be made up of a sequence of Lady Chapels dedicated to fallen Mountjoys. This impression is reinforced at every turn. The pantry has a stained glass window, the library boasts a pulpit, the scullery has two fonts and the master bedroom runs to no less than six flying buttresses.

Mountjoy Manor has a character all of its own.

I very soon became aware that I belonged to an unusual family that spurned all the conventions of normal domestic life. For instance, I hardly ever saw my parents and learned that they hardly ever saw each other. They were not so much uncaring as preoccupied. It was a happy marriage. Father had a tremendous thirst for making money and mother just had a tremendous thirst. They arranged things so that these interests were complementary rather than contradictory.

Father thrived in the City: mother toasted his success.

Sir Marcus and Lady Mountjoy: a separate togetherness.

Mother's particular gift lay in disarming any criticism of her appearance. Where people might have said that she was far too tall for a woman, they instead described her as stately; where her protruding teeth might have caused comment, it was her gracious smile that was talked about; and when her grotesque array of wigs came into the conversation, they did so as charming accessories.

Mother was a walking euphemism.

My earliest memory of her is when she blundered by mistake into the Nursery in time to see my nappy being changed. Dressed in a stunning gown of blue silk and holding a glass of champagne, she was laughing gaily to herself. Her sparkling eyes fell upon the nude form in front of her and somewhere beneath that Dolly Parton wig her maternal instinct stirred.

'Is that my child?' she asked with obvious curiosity.

'Well, it's certainly not mine!' retorted Nanny Groat.

'My Christopher!'

'Little bleeder . . . '

'My own child!' She raised her glass to me. 'Bottoms Up!'

Nanny took the advice literally and lifted me by the feet. Mother disappeared in a cloud of Johnson's Baby Powder and it was several months before our paths crossed again.

My first conscious meeting with my father was equally short. I was almost two years old and the spirit of enquiry took me on a fact-finding tour of the banqueting hall. As I was picking my way past the sarcophagi in one corner, father entered through the lychgate with a loping stride. He was a big, open-faced, distinguished-looking man with a long mane of brown hair that gave him a leonine quality.

'Who are you?' he demanded.

'Christopher . . .'

'Speak up, boy!'

'Christopher, sir.'

'*Christopher*!' He made the name sound like a notifiable disease.

'Your son, father.'

'Bless my soul!' Surprise softened his voice to a gentle growl. 'Ah, I see . . . *that* Christopher!'

And without so much as a backward glance, he vanished down the steps of the crypt where, I later discovered, he kept a telex machine for business purposes and an ice-cold plunge bath for strictly penitential moments.

If parental contact was missing from my childhood, then so was sibling rivalry. It was a long time before I knew that I had a brother and even longer before I actually met him. Barnaby is twelve years older than me but he made it seem more like a hundred and twelve. Everything about him suggested a pillar of Victorian rectitude. Because he allowed nobody to trespass upon his sense of self-importance, he pretended that I did not exist and kept well clear of any brotherly claims that I might make.

Davinia, by contrast, was willing enough to acknowledge me because I rescued her from being the baby of the family and came in useful as target practice for her malevolent wiles. Luckily, since she is five years older than me, she was away at school most of the time and it was only during her holidays that I had to endure the sort of torment that she meted out.

One of her attacks on me led to a second christening. It took place in the Blue Bathroom. I was barely four years old – an impressionable age, I always feel – and Nanny Groat was giving me my usual evening sluice while singing her usual sea shanty. She had made me stand up on my infant pins so that she could soap my endearing little Chinese wrestler pot belly and its environs.

Suddenly, without warning and without mercy, the door was flung open and we were invaded by an army of giggle and screech. Leading the charge, of course, was Davinia, all pigtail, teeth-brace and indiscriminate malice. At her heels was a pack of Visigoth schoolfriends bent on rape, pillage and the wanton destruction of my tiny ego.

I was male: they were female. Only one thing appeased their lustful curiosity and they jostled for a private viewing.

Davinia pointed a sisterly finger and laughed.

'Look at it!' she screamed in derision. 'Small, pink and wrinkly. Just like Great-Aunt Lucy.'

They were still chanting the name with glee as Nanny drove them from the bathroom with a mouthful of abuse and a loofah.

Covered in Camay, Great-Aunt Lucy was red with embarrassment and tingling with righteous indignation. Nanny was able to wash away the soap but the name stuck. Even when it was no longer small, pink and wrinkly, it remained, albeit de-hyphenated, what it had been called in the Blue Bathroom.

When time passed and puberty duly delivered its two dangling companions, Davinia – inevitably – had to name them as well.

'How are Great Aunt Lucy and the two boys?'

Little did she realize that she was sealing the fate of a thousand members of her sex with her gibe. Destiny was to call me. Great Aunt Lucy and the two boys had the mark of privilege and the lustre of high definition performance.

They were to travel the world in search of amorous adventure.

The Mountjoy Memoirs tell their story.

Such then is the family into which I was born. A busy father obsessed with high finance and the good name of the Mountjoys. An alcoholic mother who could pass the height requirement for the Harlem Globetrotters. A pompous prig of a brother with a personality so rigid that he could have rented it out as scaffolding. And a predatory sister who had mastered all the arts of slow torture.

They were my nearest and dearest. Occasional visitors to my life. Random passers-by. They inhabited another world that I was not permitted to enter. It made me feel lonely.

The yawning gap that was left by my absentee family was filled by Nanny Groat, who was father, mother, brother and sister rolled into one. She was also friend, protector, mentor, entertainer and wise owl.

During my formative years, Nanny Groat was my salvation.

'May I ask you a question, Nanny?'

'No.'

'What's the difference between boys and girls?'

'Boys are kinder.'

'Yes, but what's different about the way they *look*?'

'Boys have kinder faces.'

'That's not what I meant.'

'Go to sleep.'

'Tell me a story first.'

'Not a bleeding chance!'

'A *sea* story.'

'Once upon a time . . . '

It always worked. Nanny could not resist the call of the sea.

Her whole life had been a saga of thwarted ambition. She longed to be a sailor and ran off to sea as soon as she was old enough, but she only got as far as Mountjoy Manor. There, at least, she could indulge her fantasies. Very few employers would have let their Nanny wear – as ours did – denims, gumboots, dark blue sweater and a peaked cap. And what other family would have sanctioned a daily allowance of grog? Nanny Groat was in love with the sea. If you held her to your ear, you could hear the waves roar.

The bathroom was her natural element.

'What will it be today, Nanny?'

'Guess.'

'Sinking the *Bismarck*?'

'We did that last week.'

'Raising the *Mary Rose*?'

'Not enough action.'

'Leading the mutiny on the *Bounty*?'

'Not enough blood.'

'Then what?'

'Fighting the Spanish Sodding Armada!'

Other children played with plastic ducks in their baths. I was much more likely to be sharing my water with a scale-model of the *Scharnhorst*. Nothing was left out. We sailed with Magellan, explored with Columbus, discovered with Cook and served under Nelson. We even stood on the bridge beside Jack Hawkins.

My childhood was a voyage of delight on the seven seas of naval history. Nanny Groat entered into the spirit of it all. She would toss her cap in the air when we sank an enemy vessel and I can still see the tears streaming down her weather-beaten old face as the *Titanic* went under with its orchestra playing bravely to the last. We were true shipmates and she would wrap a tattooed arm around me whenever she burst into a sea shanty.

Though my early years were spent before the mast, my education was not neglected. I was encouraged to ask any question and Nanny would answer it in her gruff and direct way.

'Where do babies come from, Nanny?'

'Beds.'

'What's sex?'

'Something men worry about.'
'How do you have an orgasm?'
'Join the Navy.'
'Why doesn't Davinia like me?'
'She's your sister.'
'Will *you* ever get married, Nanny?'
'Be quiet and suck your Fisherman's Friend . . . '

There are not many children who have two mothers and I was deeply fond of them both. I keep their memory alive with a treasured object which I bought in an antique shop in Portsmouth. Whenever I look at that ship in a bottle, I think of Nanny Groat and Lady Mountjoy at one and the same time. Both revelled in a liquid environment.

I pass now to an event of crucial importance that occurred on my fifth birthday. I was summoned to have tea with both my parents, a momentous occasion because the last time they had done anything together had been nine months before my birth. Nanny Groat schooled me carefully beforehand. I was to call my father 'sir' and to approach my mother with a silver tray balanced on my left hand so that I could receive her empty glass. Moreover, I was neither to show nor expect any overt sign of affection. The Mountjoys have a strict code in these matters.

The rehearsals proved to be in vain. When I presented myself in the withdrawing room, my parents had withdrawn. Lying on the coffee table beside a discarded Afro wig and a copy of the *Financial Times* was a white envelope bearing my name. I opened it at once to find a small but engaging birthday card signed by my mother and countersigned, in his absence, by one of father's secretaries. A pencilled message explained that mother had gone off to the opening ceremony for a new distillery and that Father had flown to Hong Kong to inspect some of his merchant banks.

Both parents, said the pencil, were looking forward to seeing me at my next birthday.

I was disappointed but not really surprised. Slipping the card into my pocket, I was about to leave when I noticed something at the far end of the room. At first glance, it looked like a life-size effigy of a Catholic saint. Then it spoke.

'Hello . . . ' The voice was light and frail.

'Hello,' I replied.

'You must be Christopher.'

'Yes.'

'I'm *so* pleased to meet you at last,' she said, moving slowly towards me. 'I am Great-Aunt Lucy.'

My namesake blushed unseen and my face turned the colour of the Blue Bathroom. She appraised me carefully through smiling eyes.

'So *you* are dear Christopher! The youngest of the Mountjoys. Yes, you are exactly as I had imagined.'

'I'm afraid that mother and father are not here,' I apologized. 'But I'll tell them that you called.'

'I did not come to see your parents,' she rejoined with a hint of asperity. 'Why should I visit them when they never visit me? No, I am here to see you, Christopher.'

'Me?' I was both honoured and baffled.

'It's your birthday.'

'Yes, but – '

'Someone from the family should help you to celebrate it.' She took a tiny, perfumed envelope from her handbag. 'Happy birthday!'

'Thank you.'

I took the proffered envelope and opened it to release the full fragrance. The card inside sported a golden number five above a cricket bat, a dartboard and a racing cycle. She had penned her love and best wishes to me in minute writing. I was touched.

'Thank you,' I repeated. 'Thank you very much.'

'It was my last chance to introduce myself, you see. I mean, you have reached school age now. You will soon be sent away and then I should have no opportunity at all of getting to know you.'

As Davinia had said, Great-Aunt Lucy was indeed small, pink and wrinkly but those adjectives gave only a partial description. It was her skin I noticed first. It was as soft and delicate as rice paper with a gentle sheen that gave her a saintly glow. Her silver hair was swept up under a feathered hat and pearl earrings matched her necklace. Dressed in a suit of pale green with shoes and handbag in a darker shade, she looked ancient but immaculate. I liked her.

'Do sit down,' I piped.

'Thank you, Christopher.'

When we sat beside each other on the settee, she reached out and took my infant hand in hers. There was, after all, a member of the Mountjoy family who actually wanted to spend time with me. I felt reassured.

'I wish that we'd met before, Great-Aunt Lucy.'

'So do I, so do I. But you know how unreliable your parents are about visitors. Besides, I am abroad several months of the year.'

'Where?'

'A variety of places. I have never enjoyed the best of health, you see, and I tend to follow the sun. In my younger days, I would stay at all the famous spas and take the waters. Now I just settle for somewhere hot and quiet and civilized.' Her grasp tightened a little. 'Are you a truthful boy, Christopher?'

'I try to be.'

'Yes, I'm sure you do.' She gazed at me in silence for a few minutes as if weighing up a decision. 'I, too, try to be honest with people and I shall certainly be honest with you. I hope that this does not come as a shock but I detest your brother.'

'Barnaby?'

'An odious and complacent individual.'

'Oh.'

'Also, I have a profound dislike of your sister.'

'Davinia?'

'All that giggling at others' expense. All that meanness.'

'She is mean sometimes,' I agreed.

'That's why it must be you.'

'What must?'

'You'll see,' she purred. 'Were you pleased with your birthday presents?'

'I didn't really get any. Except that marlinspike from Nanny Groat. Mother and father don't believe in presents.'

'I was referring to *my* gifts.' She laughed lightly at my puzzled expression. 'On the birthday card,' she explained.

'The cricket bat, dartboard and racing cycle?'

'All wrapped up and waiting for you in my car.'

'Thank you! That's so kind of you!' I enthused.

She squeezed my hand. 'Tell me about yourself, Christopher.'

'What would you like to know, Great-Aunt?'

'Everything.'

'Everything?'

'The story of your sweet little life. Tell me.'

And so I did. Omitting only the details of the christening in the Blue Bathroom, I told her all that had happened to me in five full years at Mountjoy Manor. She nodded and sighed and frowned and chuckled. Whatever decision she made earlier, I was somehow ratifying it with my autobiography. When I had finished, she kissed me gently on the forehead.

'You are the one, Christopher.'

'Am I?'

'What would you like to do most? If I could wave a magic wand and give you something, what would you ask for?'

'The chance to travel!' I decided.

'Travel?'

'See other countries. Meet different people.'

She regarded me levelly. 'You shall have your wish, Christopher. When the time comes, I will help you all I can. I know that you will always be grateful and that you will not forget your Great-Aunt Lucy.'

'How could I forget you!' She gave me a benign smile and stood up. 'Must you go? Let me ring for some tea.'

'We have to drive down to Heathrow.'

'But I'm having such a wonderful birthday with you.'

'I hoped you would. I'd love to stay but it's not possible. My flight leaves at eight-fifteen.' She turned on her heel. 'Come and get those presents from the car.'

And showing a surprising burst of speed, she led me out into the entrance hall and through the front door. When she reached her pink Rolls Royce, a decrepit chauffeur first helped her into the back of the vehicle then opened the boot to hand me a cricket bat, a dartboard and a racing cycle. The presents were wrapped up in striped paper and tied with blue ribbon. I was still thanking her as the Rolls Royce moved quietly down the long drive between the ranks of Lombardy poplars.

So that was her.

Great Aunt Lucy had met the real Great-Aunt Lucy.

That meeting was to change my life completely.

Chapter Two: FIRST LOVE

My amorous adventures at Eton began long before I even knew about them. During the first half I was too caught up in the novelty of the place and too preoccupied with learning the ropes to notice the impact I was having on those around me. It never occurred to me that I was arousing such a flurry of interest and I could not understand why. Before Christmas nobody was prepared to make a move and so passions remained anonymous but the New Year brought a change of tactics. The watching stage was over. Time for action.

'I thought you might care for this.'

'Thank you, sir.'

'Keats is such a marvellous poet of the senses.'

'Yes, sir.'

'I hope you enjoy reading the poems.'

'Thank you, sir.'

'Underline anything that . . . *excites* you. I will be only too happy to explain the passages to you.'

'I'm very grateful to you, sir.'

Regis was the choirmaster, a tall, thin, nervous, sensitive man with fading hair and a latticework of veins on his temples. He had an Adam's apple the size of a cricket ball and a look of such perpetual anxiety that you wanted to thrust money at him out of pity. Why this middle-aged man should intercept a young boy to whom he had never even spoken before and give him a copy of *The Complete Poems of John Keats* I did not know. It was not as if I was in the choir.

When the Adam's apple had gone bouncing off, I opened the book and read the inscription: 'A thing of beauty is a joy for ever and can you come to tea on Sunday?' Clearly, I needed advice. I talked the matter over with Gordy Hollis, my best friend at Eton. Gordy was a pale, tousle-haired cherub with an unfeigned innocence about him. We had met on our first day when another boy had tried to bully him and I had gone to his rescue. It was an attraction of opposites. While I was big, fair and athletic, Gordy was small, dark and hopeless at games. While I had the craggy good looks of a masculine Mountjoy, he had an androgynous prettiness. While I was lazy and unacademic, he was keen and intelligent.

Gordy leafed through my gift and shook his head.

'Why did old Regis give you this, Christopher?'

'Search me. I don't even like Keats.'

'Take it back and ask if you can swap it for Roger McGough.'

'What do I do about the invitation to tea?'

'Depends how hungry you are on Sunday.'

'Be serious, Gordy!' I chided. 'What would you do?'

He considered for a moment then shrugged. 'Go, probably.'

'You didn't see Regis when he gave me the book. He had this sort of wild and desperate look about him.'

'All choirmasters are like that.'

'Then there's the other thing,' I continued. 'I don't really want him to spout Keats at me. Poetry always brings me out in spots.'

'Keats shouldn't,' he said knowledgeably. 'He wrote some jolly good stuff. I'll say this for Regis. He's got taste.' He peered at me. 'Surprised you don't like poetry, though. I've always thought you had a poetic look to you in some ways. When you're asleep, you're amazingly like the dying Chatterton.'

Gordy had solved my problem. Since I had qualms about going alone to Regis for tea and quotations, I decided to take a friend along for moral support. While I tucked into the food, Gordy and Regis could talk about the Romantic Poets to their hearts' content.

It did not quite work out like that. When Sunday came and we presented ourselves at his lodgings, Regis threw open the door with a smile of anticipatory delight. His face froze when he saw that I had company and his Adam's apple went into orbit around his neck. I have never seen a man look so betrayed and uncomfortable.

'This is Gordy Hollis, sir,' I introduced. 'He likes Keats as well.'

'Does he?' grunted Regis.

'My favourite poet, sir,' said Gordy with evident sincerity.

'I hope you don't mind my bringing a friend, sir.'

'You'd better come in,' muttered our host.

The room into which we were conducted was large, comfortable and unrepentantly old-fashioned. Although it was still day, the curtains had been drawn and a standard lamp supplied the only light. Books and newspapers were scattered all over the two armchairs so that the leather sofa was the only place to sit. On the turntable of the music centre, Ravel's Bolero was throbbing soulfully away.

'Sit here,' said Regis, clearing everything off the two armchairs. 'I'll bring tea in.'

'Thank you, sir,' I said.

'Thank you, sir,' echoed Gordy. 'What I like most about Keats is – '

But Regis had gone off to the kitchen and we heard him banging about in there for some time. When he returned, he gave us tea and cakes and sat palpitating on the sofa while Gordy held forth about the virtues of *La Belle Dame Sans Merci*. The choirmaster cleared the tea things away as soon as we had finished then hustled us out with some gabbled excuse about having a headache. As we walked away from the building, we heard Wagner replace Ravel.

'That was short and sweet,' observed Gordy.

'Why do you suppose he was wearing that track suit?' I wondered.

'Maybe he expected to do some running.'

Innocence is truly its own best protection.

Regis did not invite me to tea again or bestow any more poetry books on me. He was often seen, alone and palely loitering, outside our dormitory but apart from a nocturnal serenade sung in high falsetto, he made no other frontal approach. I was grateful.

As he backed off, others moved in. Bouquets of flowers began to arrive from various sources and an unknown soul in torment wrote to tell me that he and I had made exquisite love for the last thirty-five consecutive nights and that he could never know true happiness unless I consented to be his. Advised by Gordy, I laid low and did nothing. The flowers eventually stopped and my hidden admirer ran out of steam before he made it to the half-century.

While I could cope with the blatant, I was still not experienced enough to perceive and neutralize the subtle. When no less a person than the Captain of the House befriended me, therefore, I was happily blind to what might be coming.

It was a fine day in March and we sauntered by the river.

'I've been thinking, Mountjoy . . . '

'Yes, Williamson?'

'It might be rather amusing if I did a portrait of you.'

'Of me?' I was flattered. His artistic talent was considerable and some of his work was on display in our corridors. 'I couldn't put you to the trouble,' I said.

'No trouble,' he replied, casually.

When I had seen Justin Williamson on my first day at Eton, I had been quite over-awed. He was a lanky but poised young man with a flashy handsomeness and an easy assurance. Chosen from among the self-electing prefects of Library to be Captain of the House, he was a minor god. Power, influence and kudos encircled his head like concentric haloes. And it was this ethereal figure, this autocrat, this paragon who was offering to do a portrait of me. I was thrilled.

Gordy was frankly envious. As we played chess together

one day, he told me that he would love to be the subject of a painting by Williamson.

'Some of his work has been *sold*, Christopher.'

'Check!' I said, moving my queen in for the kill.

'In proper art galleries. For money.'

'Check!'

'Perhaps he'll sell the portrait of you.'

'Check!'

'How would you like to hang in the Tate?'

'Checkmate!'

Chess was very much the fashion that half. Many of us carried pocket sets for impromptu challenges and games were played with high seriousness. As a rule, Gordy could beat me easily.

'You've won!' he complained in surprise.

'Only because you weren't concentrating.'

'Let's have another game.'

'Later, Gordy. I have my first sitting with Williamson now.'

'Good luck!'

With my chess set in my hand, I ran off to my appointment.

Williamson's room had the authentic feel of an artist's studio. Framed prints of the Great Masters were everywhere and examples of his own work complemented them. Books, magazines, pads of cartridge paper, masks, statuettes, collages and a range of artist's materials were scattered about with carefree abandon. In the middle of it all was the Renaissance man himself, my House Captain, my friend, my hero.

It did not strike me as at all odd that he should be wearing nothing but a multi-coloured silk dressing gown and a pair of velvet slippers. Artists are by nature idiosyncratic. Evidently, it was Williamson's habit to dress up like a bird of paradise while he painted.

'I'll just lock this door, Mountjoy,' he said, turning the key in the lock. 'We don't want to be interrupted.'

'Of course not, Williamson.'

'How are you feeling?'

'Fine, fine . . .'

'Good. I can't work with a nervous model.'

'Oh, I'm not at all nervous,' I volunteered amiably.

'I knew that you wouldn't be.'

With a hand that smelled more of Eau Savage than oil paint, he guided me to the far side of the room between the sofa and the window.

'I'd like you where the light falls on you,' he explained then went back to his easel to appraise me critically. Sunlight streamed in to gild my hair. I smiled happily as if I were having my photograph taken. 'Yes, that's more or less perfect,' he added.

'Ready when you are!' I called out obligingly.

'But you haven't taken your things off yet.'

'What?'

'I see you as a young Atlas with the world on your shoulder.' He picked up a large metal globe with several dents in it. 'It will be a nude portrait of Strength, Character and Manliness.'

'Really?' I was impressed.

'Now don't waste time or we shall miss the light.'

Though I did not exactly feel strong, characterful or manly at that moment, I put down my chess set and undressed quickly, throwing my things on the sofa. Williamson regarded me. His intake of breath must have been heard in Windsor.

'Magnificent! Truly magnificent!'

'Thank you,' I said modestly.

'Just hold this . . .'

Handing me the globe, he made me experiment with various positions until he found one that he liked. I was crouched down with my feet apart and my muscles tensed to take the weight of the world. The globe was cold and heavy on my shoulder but I did not mind. I told myself that discomfort was part of the price I had to pay for the honour of being able to work with a great artist.

Williamson began his preliminary sketch. Because my

face was in profile to him, I could not see what he was doing but I sensed that he was drawing swiftly and fluently. His breathing then seemed to get heavier and by the time he dabbed the first touch of paint on the canvas, he sounded like an industrial vacuum cleaner with a bad case of laryngitis.

When he spoke, his voice was octaves lower than usual.

'Are you happy at Eton, Mountjoy?'

'Very happy, Williamson.'

'Am I anything to do with that happiness?'

'Oh yes!'

The vacuum cleaner came on again for a few minutes.

I was now aching in every joint and feeling an early warning of cramp in my left leg. To take my mind off my suffering, I gazed down at my chess set on the sofa and thought about my recent game with Gordy Hollis. My head was still full of gambits when the conversation resumed. Williamson had obviously spotted the chess set.

'Do you ever play with yourself?'

'Frequently,' I confessed. 'You have to keep your hand in.'

'And have you ever . . . played with anyone else?'

'I do it all the time.'

'Indeed?' Surprise was tinged with relief. 'With whom?'

'Gordy Hollis, mostly. I played with him earlier on.'

'And did he play with you?'

'Of course.'

'It hasn't left you . . . tired out, has it?'

'No,' I said blithely. 'I can keep it up all day without tiring.'

'Which do you prefer? To do it alone or with someone else?'

'Oh, it's much more fun with a partner, Williamson.'

'Why?'

'Because of the competition!'

He became technical. 'And how – exactly – do you like to do it?'

'Slowly. I think before every move. You don't make

mistakes that way and it's also a kind of tease for the other chap.'

More hoovering followed. 'Would you like to play with me?'

'Very much, Williamson.'

'And will you promise to go slowly and tease me?'

'Yes. Until I get my hands on your first piece, anyway.'

'Play with me, Mountjoy!' he pleaded.

'When do you suggest?' I asked cheerfully.

'Now.'

'Right this minute?'

'Now!' I heard the swish of silk as the dressing gown was discarded.

'Have you finished the portrait already?'

'NOW!!!!'

The animal frenzy of his howl made me look around at him and I blenched. With the brush still in his hand, he was standing there naked and pawing the ground. He had painted me into a corner.

His was a game of weightier consequence than chess and he was ready to make the first move. Casting the brush aside, he came lunging at me with arms open. In sheer terror, I threw the globe up into the air and backed away. Fate interceded on my behalf. As Williamson closed in on me, the globe struck the ceiling and split in two, one of the hemispheres spinning down until it caught the Captain of the House at the very tip of his arousal.

He yelled in agony and fell to the carpet with his world in ruins around him. Grabbing my clothes and my chess set, I made an excuse and left. He continued to screech with pain and drew no consolation from the fact that he had just set a precedent in being the only man in medical history to have been circumcized by the equator.

Williamson and I were poles apart from that day on.

Easter that year will always stand clear in my mind. Apart from its marking my first experience of conventional family life, it was the time when I fell deeply and hopelessly in love.

Gordy had invited me to spend a week of the holiday with him and he was there with his parents to give me a cordial welcome when I arrived at the station. It took me some while to adjust to the fact that Mr and Mrs Hollis actually seemed to enjoy each other's company enough to want to be together. Also, that they were ready to spend time with their son. Such phenomena were unknown at Mountjoy Manor. I had seen neither of my parents since Christmas.

Mr Hollis was a warm, friendly extrovert with trendy clothes and a professional footballer hairstyle. His wife had the kind face and exaggerated brightness of a *Playschool* presenter. On the drive back to Kenilworth, they put me completely at ease and told me how pleased they were that Gordy had such a good friend at Eton. He had told them all about me, they said, and he felt that he owed me a lot. To show willing, I weighed in with some stuff about the debt that I owed to their son and it all seemed to go down very well.

They lived in a large, modern bungalow in a wooded road near the famous castle. Because Mr Hollis was manager of a factory that made electrical goods, the place was full of appliances and gadgets of all kinds. Gordy had a lot of fun showing them off to me. We were in the lounge playing with the computer when my life suddenly underwent a radical change of direction.

Rosemary Anne walked in.

'Hello, Christopher. I'm Gordy's twin sister.'

'Hello.'

'Hope you enjoy your stay.'

'Thanks.'

'See you later. I have to go and ride.'

That was all that was said but it was more than enough. My heart would for ever belong in the Hollis lounge beside that computer. Euphoria gave me a vapid grin. I was in love.

Rosemary Anne was the most beautiful creature I had ever seen. Though she bore a striking resemblance to her twin brother, she was in many ways very unlike him. She was taller, slimmer, darker, more poised and she had dimples in her cheeks that he could not hope to match. Again, she had more confidence than Gordy, more sense of purpose.

What set her apart from any girl I had ever met before was her pleasant and easy manner. As I stood there at the window and watched her striding across the paddock, I realized what a disservice Davinia and her friends had done to the female sex. By her constant persecution of me over the years, my sister had left me with a very jaundiced view of girlhood.

At one stroke, Rosemary Anne Hollis altered that.

'Do you ride, Christopher?'

'What?' I came out of my reverie. 'Oh. No, I don't.'

'That's a pity,' said Gordy. 'You could've had a go on Tammy.'

'Tammy?'

'Rosemary Anne's horse. I'm sure she would've let you.'

'Actually,' I heard myself saying, 'I have done a bit of riding and I'd love a go on Tammy.' Through the window, I saw a grey pony trot over to Rosemary Anne. 'I bet your sister is a good horsewoman.'

'Come and see for yourself.'

He led me across the hall to her bedroom. It was a shrine. Two whole walls were covered with rosettes that she had won at various shows and I counted over a dozen cups and shields on the chest of drawers. Posters of horses filled the rest of the available wall space. I was particularly interested in the photographs of Rosemary Anne in competition and my love for her burned inside me. When I saw one photograph of her rising in the saddle as the horse cleared a jump, something darker than love began to smoulder. It made my thighs tremble and my cheeks go red.

For all the emphasis on riding, however, the room still remained a boudoir – private, cared for, very feminine. It told me a lot about Rosemary Anne and even more about myself. I wanted her to be mine for the rest of my life. She was everything to me.

I passed the bulk of the week in a daze. Though I had an enjoyable time with Gordy, my mind was always on his sister. On her beauty, her sense of humour, her riding skill, her cheerfulness, her robustness, her intelligence, her body. When I was alone with him, it was his resemblance to Rosemary Anne that I noticed. Alone with her, I was in heaven.

'Pass me the bridle.'

'This?' I asked, picking up a thick leather object.

'No, silly!' she scolded with a laugh. 'That's a cavesson. I thought you'd ridden before, Christopher.'

'It was some time ago,' I mumbled.

We were in the stable and Rosemary Anne was tacking up her pony for me. Tammy stood there obediently as her red numnah and her saddle were put on. She looked sleek and well-groomed. I kept patting her neck to build up my confidence and to try to establish a friendly relationship with her. It was several years since I had been anywhere near a horse.

Rosemary Anne led Tammy out into the paddock.

'I'll just warm her up for you, Christopher.'

'Oh. Thank you.'

As soon as I saw the animal in action, I regretted my folly. Tammy was a four-legged rocket. Urged on by Rosemary Anne, she galloped around the perimeter of the field at a furious pace. She was then reined in to a canter and aimed at the first of a series of jumps. She sailed over it with ease, cleared three more, then headed back towards me.

'She's all yours, Christopher.'

'I don't want to jump her.'

'But she loves it.'

I struggled into the saddle and Rosemary Anne adjusted the stirrups for me. Then she patted Tammy firmly on the rump and we were away. We went at a steady canter around the paddock with me clinging on for dear life. I was bounced up and down so hard that I thought I would split in two. Then Tammy swung round to address one of the jumps. I heaved on the reins but she ignored all my attempts to control her. Pounding towards a three-foot pole, she chose her moment to take off and rose majestically. It was the most exhilarating feeling, almost as if I were flying through the air of my own volition.

And I was. Tammy had unseated me. While she went on to the next jump, I hit the ground and did a couple of somersaults. Rosemary Anne was beside me in an instant to help me up and offer sympathy.

'Are you alright?'

'I think so.'

'You were going well until you came off.'

'Thanks.'

'Try again,' she encouraged.

'Er, no. That'll do me for today.'

'Are you sure?'

Tammy came walking over to us and nuzzled against Rosemary Anne's shoulder. I patted the animal to show that I bore no grudges and then I tried to walk. My legs were encased in lead and aching violently.

'Saddle-sore?' asked Rosemary Anne with a grin.

'Just a little.'

'I've got some ointment up at the house. Would you like some?'

'Please.'

'I'll rub it in for you.'

'No, no, that's okay,' I said quickly. 'I can manage.'

She laughed at my embarrassment and then led Tammy towards the stable again. The riding lesson was over. It had been an ordeal for me but I felt that a small bond had been forged with Rosemary Anne.

That made everything worthwhile.

Late that night, I lay in bed and reviewed my holiday. I had come to spend time with a friend and found a girl that I wanted to marry. It had given my life a whole new meaning and resonance and purpose. Before I came to Kenilworth again, I promised myself, I would learn to ride properly. If the way to Rosemary Anne's heart was through her pony, then I would act accordingly.

As I turned over on to my back, I felt the full effects of the soreness and winced. The ointment that she had given me had been very soothing and I decided to apply some more. Taking care not to wake Gordy whose room I was sharing, I eased myself out from under the sheets and moved slowly towards the door. My muscles had hardened completely now and every step was an effort but I knew that relief was waiting for me in the bathroom cabinet.

I let myself out silently into the darkness of the hall and shut the door gently behind me. There was a light on in the bathroom and I waited until I heard the toilet flush. After a short while, the door opened to reveal a vision of pure delight.

Framed in the doorway for one fleeting but magical moment, was Rosemary Anne. Naked, unashamed and quite unselfconscious. I had never seen anything so wonderful. Her long, slender body was just starting to take on the shape of a woman. Soft, sloping breasts had formed and her hips were rounding out. The skin had a translucent quality and her dark hair gleamed.

She switched off the light and strolled off to let herself into her own bedroom. As I gazed after her, I knew that I would love her for the rest of my life and that nobody would ever compare with her.

My love did not confine itself to an emotional upsurge. There were physical responses of all kinds. I felt my cheeks redden again and my thighs tremble. My fatigue fell away from me and my whole body was vibrant with desire. Though I had no idea whatsoever how to do it, I wanted to possess her and make her mine in every way.

When I looked down at Great Aunt Lucy, I saw something else.

I was growing up.

Chapter Three: DEATHS AND ENTRANCES

There was something sinister about Dexter. Everybody said so. It was difficult to put your finger on it but it was there. And it was an endless source of speculation among the Lower Boys. Quentin Dexter was our housemaster, a dark, thin, saturnine man of middle years with mottled skin and eyes of different colours above a stage villain moustache. He had the slovenly appearance of the true academic but you felt that he was hiding something beneath the surface. A secret sorrow, perhaps. A gnawing doubt. A burden of guilt. Another persona.

I disliked him intensely. He made my flesh creep.

In view of this, I was very alarmed that summer when Dexter sent for me during a Latin period. A housemaster does not usually haul a boy out of a lesson unless it is a matter of some importance. I hoped that it would not be about my work. That was my Achilles' heel.

'Come in, Mountjoy . . . '

'Thank you, sir.'

'Close the door behind you.'

'Yes, sir.'

'Now sit down over here.'

'Yes, sir.'

I sat in front of his desk with some trepidation. For a short interview, he would have kept me standing. Evidently, there was to be a thorough examination of my crime sheet. I braced myself.

The room was an amiable clutter of books, papers, magazines and faded prints and Dexter seemed entirely at home in this donnish habitat. As he spoke out of the side of his mouth, his moustache assumed the diagonal. Not certain on which eye to concentrate, I moved between blue and green at random.

'I have heard some disturbing news,' he began.

'Have you, sir?'

'I felt I had to speak to you at once.'

The solemnity in his voice and the intensity of his two-tone stare confirmed my suspicions. I was on the carpet because of my scholastic shortcomings.

'Mountjoy,' he continued, 'it pains me to say this . . . '

'If it's about the French essay, sir, I can explain that.'

'French essay?' He was politely baffled.

'Ah, then it must be about my Chemistry experiment. I'm dreadfully sorry about the mishap, sir. My father will be more than ready to pay for the damage I inadvertently did to the laboratory.'

'I have just spoken with your father,' he said pointedly.

'Oh!' Tremors began in earnest. 'How, er . . . how is he, sir?'

'Distressed. As one might expect. Very distressed.'

'Of course, sir.'

'It came as something of a shock to him.'

'Mr Croxley must takc soine of the blame,' I argued. 'He's tried to take us too far too fast. That's why I'm floundering with Algebra, sir. I'm sure that I'll get the hang of it.'

'I'll bear that in mind,' he said with lugubrious concern then stood up behind the desk. 'You will leave tomorrow.'

'*Leave*!' The tremors made a bid for earthquake status.

'For home, Mountjoy.'

'Must I, sir?'

'It is only seemly.'

'At least give me a second chance. I've actually started to enjoy German now I've worked out where the verb goes.'

'You leave in the morning,' he droned.

'But I *like* it here!'

'It has all been arranged. I have talked with the headmaster. I have even had a word with the Provost. They concur.'

'I see.' The earthquake had now reached Californian dimensions. It was time to accept defeat graciously. 'Before I depart from Eton, sir, I would like you to know how much I've enjoyed it here.'

'Indeed?' He plucked at his moustache. 'When I was your age, I used to loathe the place. Eton is the prisoner of its glorious past. You keep stubbing your toe against history. I was so unhappy here. I hated fagging. I hated being beaten.' The blue eye filmed over with sadness. 'To be honest, I sometimes wonder why I ever came back to teach here.'

His green eye gazed down wistfully at his desk and I noted for the first time the framed photograph of his wife. She was a short, stout, bosomy creature with a severe hairstyle and a plain face made even plainer by her expression of total contempt for the photographer. Dexter ran a finger gently across the top of the frame before pulling himself together.

'Goodbye, Mountjoy.'

'Goodbye, sir,' I said, standing up.

'My commiserations . . . ' He offered his hand.

'Thank you.' It was giving him no pleasure to expel me. I was grateful for that and returned the handshake. His palm felt clammy. 'Just one thing, sir . . . '

'Yes?'

'Well, I would like to know what did it.'

'They will tell you that when you reach home.'

'Was it my History or did my unequal struggle against Geometry turn the scales?' There was no discernible response. 'In that case, it must be my Physics that did it. Was it, sir?'

'No. It was your Biology.'

'But we don't take Biology, sir.'

'I was referring to hereditary circumstances.' He made a bungled attempt to introduce sympathy into his voice.

'Don't you understand, Mountjoy? There's been a death in your family.'

The earthquake gave a repeat performance. A *death?* Whose? Had father drowned in the ice-cold plunge bath? Had mother finally had one drink too many? Could it be Barnaby? Davinia, even? I was now confronted with a fate worse than being thrown out of Eton.

'May I ask who it was, sir?'

'Need we go into ghoulish detail, Mountjoy?'

'Please, sir. This is important.'

'Very well. If you insist . . .'

'I do, sir.'

'It was your Great-Aunt Lucy.'

The blow left me dizzy. She was the one person I had not even considered. I was sad, confused and desperately hurt. I sensed that a great value had just dropped out of my life.

'You had better lie down,' advised my housemaster. I began to lower myself to the threadbare carpet. 'No, not here! On your bed.' His tone took on a sinister inflection. '*Alone*!'

'Yes, sir.'

He showed me to the door and opened it. 'Once again, accept my condolences. And do give my regards to Sir Marcus.'

I nodded and walked out into a world that now seemed poorer as a result of the death of a small, pink and wrinkly old lady.

The funeral was a quiet affair. Not that funerals are exactly noisy on any occasion but this was a particularly muted one. It was small, dignified and affecting. Just like Great-Aunt Lucy herself. She had in fact passed away ten days earlier somewhere in the south of France but bureaucratic wrangling had delayed the return of her body to her native land. Compassionate leave had been bestowed upon me so that I could accompany mother to the funeral. We were, as it turned out, the only representatives of the Mountjoy family.

Mother wore a stupendous dress of black taffeta that rustled as she walked and had a small pocket discreetly sewn into its folds for her hip flask. Her black straw hat possessed such a wide, dipping brim that it was impossible to get close to her without serious facial injury. A black veil, a black handbag, black patent leather shoes and gloves of black lace completed the outfit. For once she dispensed with a wig and wore her own handsome greying hair.

The drive to the church gave us time for a rare chat.

'How did it happen, mother?'

'Happen?' She took a swig from the hip flask. 'What?'

'Great-Aunt Lucy.'

'She died.'

'Yes, but *how*?'

'The same way we all die, Christopher. Completely alone.'

'There must have been a cause of death.'

'Poor Lucy never had time to tell me what it was.'

'A doctor must have signed a certificate.'

'Darling,' she sighed, 'who can trust anything a Frenchman says?'

'Is it simply a case of age?'

'I have no idea how old the French doctor was.'

'Not *him*, mother!'

'Then whom?'

'Her!'

She pondered. 'Yes. Very possible. Anno domini trouble. She reached the end of her allotted span and the Great Traffic Warden in the Sky gave her a ticket. More than likely.' She paused to show her respect as we passed the village Wine Shop. 'So characteristic of dear Lucy, though. To be so punctual. Everything in her life was so neat and tidy.'

'I'm not quite with you, mother.'

'She died on her eighty-first birthday.'

'Oh!' It added new poignance. 'What a terrible shame!'

'I call it superb timing, Christopher,' said mother robustly. 'To combine two such important events in the calendar of your life. It makes for economy. People can wish you happy birthday and mourn your demise at one and the same time. I suppose that, ideally, I should have worn this dress with a funny paper hat.' The hip flask did its stuff again. 'Of course, Blanche Huntingdon went one better. She had her birthday, her wedding and her death on the same day. I can still see that mingled look of elation and despair on her husband's face. He wasn't sure whether to kiss the bride or send for the undertaker. But he got over it. I remember him telling me that it may have been a short marriage but it was a consistently happy one.' She peered out of the window as the car stopped. 'We're here. Let's go and get it over with!'

'Yes, mother.'

'Eighty-one! It's a fine age.'

'She was a fine woman.'

'You met her, dear?'

'Only once. But that was enough to make me very fond of her.'

'Lucy was rather like that.'

The chauffeur had got out to open the door for us. Mother stepped out of the car and handed him the hip flask as she went past.

If the history of the Miniature Parish Church ever comes to be written then St Saviour's, Hampton Magna, will qualify for at least a chaper to itself. It is tiny and is really no more than a side-chapel with ideas above its station. As chief mourners, mother and I sat at the front. The pews were so close together that her hat kept the two rows behind us completely clear, thus heightening our sense of isolation. There were ten other mourners, all elderly gentlemen looking spry and immaculate, but we knew none of them.

I wondered if they had been rented like a marquee.

When I saw the coffin on its trolley, my heart shuddered. It was so small and defenceless. I had to look away for the rest of the service. The vicar had obviously been hand-chosen for the job. He was an ancient, balding gnome who fitted perfectly into the minute pulpit. There was nothing shrunken about his oration, however. He paid tribute to Great-Aunt Lucy in expansive terms and waxed lyrical about her sterling virtues. Though I had only met her that once, I recognized the accuracy of his remarks.

Mother wept copiously throughout and worked her way through a stockpile of black lace handkerchieves before moving on to Kleenex tissues. Other sniffles came from behind us when the coffin was rolled down the aisle towards the narrow slit in the stone that posed as a door. Further tears were shed at the graveside as Great-Aunt Lucy, a lifelong traveller, made her final journey south. We mumbled a few words of thanks to the vicar then headed for the car.

The woman I had met on my own birthday had now taken leave of me on her own. It made our relationship at once symmetrical and sad. What I did not appreciate at the time, of course, was that every exit is also an entrance. In going through the final door herself, she was opening a hundred doors for me. In losing her, I was only starting to gain what she had to offer me.

It was not until the black limousine turned into the drive of Mountjoy Manor that mother regained her composure. She had found the experience as harrowing as I had and was wishing that she had brought a flask for the other hip. She squeezed my arm for comfort and struck up a conversation.

'When do you start school, dear?'

'I've been at school for a number of years, mother.'

'Indeed?'

'At the moment, I'm at Eton.'

'Oh, that's nice. Your father went there. In fact, it was thanks to Eton that we got married.'

'Was it?'

'Indirectly. We were at a shooting party somewhere or other. I had never met your father before and he, oddly enough, had never met me. It gave us something in common from the start. Anyway, it rained through the entire weekend and the shooting was abandoned so we amused ourselves as best we could. Your father was asked to demonstrate how the Eton Wall Game was played and I – you must appreciate that I was much younger and more impulsive then – volunteered to assist him. In the heat of the moment, things got a trifle out of hand and your father committed a gross breach of the rules. Being a man of honour, of course, he proposed to me on the spot.' The reminiscence brought a smile to her lips. 'He was playing the game, you see. And I was the Wall.'

This unscheduled insight into my parents' marriage got us as far as the front door and the car stopped to let us out. Mother halted at the top of the steps and gazed across at the motionless figure who was leaning on a rake in the middle distance.

'Who put that statue of Popeye the Sailorman in our flowerbed?'

'It's Nanny Groat.'

'Then she can take it away at once.'

'No, mother. The statue *is* Nanny Groat.'

'*Our* Nanny?' She sounded sceptical.

'She works as a gardener now.'

'Why?'

'Because we outgrew her. When there was no-one left in the Nursery for her to look after, father recycled Nanny outdoors.'

'Why am I always the last person to be told these things?'

'I don't know, mother.' I detained her as she was about to move off towards the Lounge Bar. 'Will I get a chance to see you before I leave tomorrow?'

'When do you go?'

'About ten-thirty in the morning.'.

'Probably not then, dear. I rarely get up before opening time in the warm weather. I'll say goodbye now.' She bent forward to kiss me and I ducked under her brim to avoid decapitation. 'Thank you for coming today. It meant a lot to me.'

'I was very glad that I went.'

She patted me on the head then swept into the house. The familiar clink of bottle on glass was heard almost immediately. Mother was a firm believer in the adage that one swallow does not make a summer.

I stood there trying to recover from the anguish of the funeral and from the shock of learning that I owed my existence to a chance impersonation my mother once gave of a wall. It was in this weak and vulnerable state that I was accosted by my sister. Davinia drew up in a white Jaguar that was driven by a supercilious young man with a gold chain around his neck. She spoke through the lowered window with morbid jollity.

'How did it go, Christopher? Was it creepy?'

'It was a very solemn occasion, Davinia.'

'The old bat had to die some time.'

'She was not an old bat. You should respect her memory.'

'I do,' she giggled, glancing down at my trousers.

'And don't start *that* again!'

'I'll start what I bloody well like!' she snapped defiantly then flicked a hand at her companion. 'Drive on, St John.'

The white Jaguar pulled away and went around the angle of the house. Fuming with rage, I went in through the front door and made my way to the withdrawing room. Since she had left school, Davinia had become even more rude, callous, bossy and selfish. It was impossible to see the attraction she had for any of the young men she had now started collecting.

A revving noise took me to the French windows. At the rear of the house was a small copse encircled by a gravel road that formed a natural racing track. The Jaguar was going round and round the circuit, braking at the bends and accelerating down the straits. The strange thing was that St John now seemed to be alone in the car. As each lap was completed, he was getting more and more excited and his face was one huge smile of delight. Then he suddenly rose in his seat and pressed the horn in a long, loud act of celebration.

The white Jaguar then limped to a halt. Davinia sat up

beside him and I realized what must have happened. She had fallen asleep across him and he had used his horn to rouse her.

Eton drew me back to its historic bosom and I was grateful for its compassion. It is often said that the public school system is uniquely designed to encourage a sadistic relish in its boys but I saw nothing of the sort at this difficult time. Everyone was very understanding. Gordy gave me untold sympathy, other friends kept clapping me on the back to signal their concern, and one boy assured me that he knew how I felt, having recently lost his pet rat beneath the uncaring wheels of a pantechnicon.

Official sympathy came in the form of a card from the chaplain, Reverend Charles Oates, inviting me to tea on Saturday so that he could express his condolences in person. I was touched. Charlie Chaplain, as we called him, was a most pleasant and affable young man. He was into muscular Christianity and would often be seen jogging around the playing fields or working out with heavy weights in the gymnasium. He stood in the pulpit with arms akimbo and salted his sermons with an invigorating range of sporting metaphors.

There were, however, rumours about Charlie Chaplain.

'I don't believe a word of it, Gordy,' I said.

'It's true. He has regular women visitors. At night.'

'Perhaps they're members of the Mothers' Union.'

'Not when they arrive,' he noted with a smirk. 'But they may be eligible to join by the time they leave.'

'Gordy! That's blasphemy!'

'I only know what I've heard. But tonight I'm going to see for myself. Why don't you come along as well, Christopher?'

'Where to?'

'The library. Midnight. It overlooks his lodgings. Apparently, he always comes out with some ravishing woman around then.'

I dismissed the rumour as yet another of those fictions

with which schoolboys like to sustain their fantasies but curiosity somehow took me along to the library that night. There was standing room only. The best part of a dozen boys were clustered around the window waiting for the performance to begin. We were not disappointed.

At the stroke of midnight, right on cue, the door of the chaplain's lodgings opened and he emerged stealthily. A full moon enabled us to see that he had exchanged his cassock and dog collar for a blue silk shirt open to the navel and a pair of tight black velvet trousers. Satisfied that the coast was clear, he extended a hand into the doorway and drew out a young woman who would never ever belong to a Mothers' Union. Tall, svelte and elegant, she might have stepped off the cover of a glossy magazine. When he stroked her blonde hair and gave her a tender kiss on the lips, a collective sigh went up from all of us in the dress circle. The moon was a follow-spot as he escorted her towards the main gate, pausing every so often for another moment of tenderness. When it was all over, I shook my head in disbelief but it had actually happened in front of witnesses.

A new nickname was forged that night.

Charlie Chaplain became Wild Oates.

It did rather alter my views about muscular Christianity. As I headed for the lodgings on the following afternoon, I was wondering what face to wear. It is difficult to look somnolent and grieving in the presence of an ecclesiastical Casanova. I aimed for an all-purpose expression of Christian tolerance and rang the bell.

The door soon opened and the blonde gave me a warm smile.

'Hello there!' she said huskily.

'Oh. Hello. I've come to see – '

'He'll be back directly, darling. *Do* step on in!'

'Thank you.'

I began to rue the fact that I had arrived ten minutes early for the tea and sympathy. Seen from the library, the young woman had looked slim and gorgeous. Close to, her appeal was almost overpowering. I was in a torment of embarrassment as she led me into the living room and waved to the settee. I sat down and crossed my legs gratefully.

'You *are* a sweetie, aren't you?' she observed, batting her false eyelashes at me. 'What's your name, darling?'

'Chris . . . topher,' I faltered.

'I'm Felicia. What can I offer you? G and T? Vodka and lime?'

'Er, no. Nothing for me.'

'Later, perhaps . . . I suppose you've come about Confirmation?'

'Not exactly.'

'That's how Charles and I first met, you know.'

'Is it?'

'He gave me private classes and we became confirmed friends.' She laughed at her joke then touched my shoulder with long painted fingernails. 'Seriously, darling, it's a wonderful experience! Confirmation, that is. So sexy! You kneel down and the Bishop puts his hands on your head. Divine! I liked it so much I went back three years running. That Bishop had such magic fingers.'

'Did he?'

'Let me show you what he did.'

'Well – '

'Come on. Don't be shy with Felicia.'

She pulled me from the settee and made me kneel on the carpet in front of her. The reek of her cheap perfume was captivating and I stayed there in a trance while she touched, then stroked, then massaged, then kneaded my head. Her breasts were now heaving above me and her body started to rub against me in a steady rhythm. She was making low moaning noises that were getting more and more intense. Just as I was fearing the worst, the door opened and in came the chaplain.

It took him a split second to take in the situation.

'Felix!' he roared.

'Oh, Charlie, you are a spoilsport!'

'Leave that boy alone!'

'The story of my life!' she complained, backing away. 'Someone always stops me at the wrong moment!'

'I've warned you before, Felix!'

'Don't be crossy-wossy with me, Charlie,' she cooed winningly.

'Get out!'

'I'll make it up to you, I promise.'

'You won't get the chance. This is it! The end! OUT!'

Felicia bridled. 'Well! And after all I've done for you!'

It was as if I were not there.

They went on to have the most vicious and spectacular row I have ever seen in my life. The chaplain used words that would have set the pulpit alight and his friend threw tantrum after tantrum. As they circled the room screaming abuse at each other, my erstwhile hostess pulled off her wig, eyelashes, dress, falsies, shoes and tights, hurling them into a vanity case with absolute disgust. When the chaplain demanded his jewellery back, she pulled off bracelets and bangles and rings and flung them at him in handfuls. The row soon escalated to the stage of physical violence and I opted for a tactful withdrawal.

Boys will be boys.

Eton was certainly being educative.

The letter arrived during the last week of the summer half. Gordy could see that I was thunderstruck by its contents and he took me aside at the earliest opportunity.

'Bad news, old chap?'

'Not really. It's from a London solicitor.'

'What does he have to say for himself?'

'Apparently, Great-Aunt Lucy left a will,' I explained.

'Nothing unusual in that. Par for the course.'

'I'm one of the beneficiaries, Gordy.'

'Well done! I hope the old girl has left you a fiver or two. I'll let you treat me to a strawberry mess.'

'She has left me some money, as it happens,' I admitted. 'One hundred thousand pounds.'

'*What*!' Gordy's eyes threatened to pop out of their

sockets and his jaw dropped like the back of a removal van. 'Would you repeat that figure slowly, please?'

'One hundred thousand pounds. To be received on my eighteenth birthday. What do you think of that?'

'Three cheers for Great-Aunt Lucy!'

'A hundred thousand cheers!' I exclaimed happily.

What I did not tell him was that I had also inherited a leather-bound Visitors Book and that both it and the money would be legally mine 'on his eighteenth birthday or when he comes of age, whichever is sooner'. The money was described as a 'travel bursary'. That clearly related back to our sole conversation at Mountjoy Manor. But why a Visitors Book?

And when was I supposed to come of age if not at eighteen?

As soon as it was possible, I telephoned the solicitor for some clarification. A bored, dry, unhelpful male voice told me that it had nothing to add to what was in the letter but that I could have a sight of the last will and testament of Lucy Margaret Mountjoy if I cared to call at the office in Bedford Row during business hours. What the solicitor did tell me was that I was the main beneficiary within the family circle.

Mother had inherited a collection of Oriental fans. The pink Rolls Royce had been left to father. Barnaby was now the proud owner of a marble bust of Clint Eastwood and a golf umbrella. And Davinia, my spiteful she-cat of a sister, had come by a plastic feed-tray and a dozen tins of Kit-e-Kat.

It was a will with a sense of humour.

I felt elated. Thanks to Great-Aunt Lucy, my future looked fresh and promising. She had died but I had somehow been reborn. I could not wait for the glorious moment when I would come of age.

Chapter Four: GROWING PAINS

The trouble with a public school is that it has absolutely no privacy. Growing up is something you do in front of an audience and that helps to maximize the pain of adolescent development and to refine its many humiliations. As the years passed, I certainly grew. It was not so much the sheer size that drew gasps of astonishment as its classical perfection. During the important rituals of comparison and competition, the other boys watched in disbelief as it grew swiftly through its Doric Phase to its Ionic Glory and thence on to its full Corinithian splendour.

After showers or swimming there would be fights to see who would carry my towel for me and I lost count of the number of offers to wash my underwear. It was quite bewildering. I was in possession of something unusual and desirable but I had no idea what to do with it.

Fleet was the first to spot the commercial potentialities.

'Can I have a word with you, Mountjoy?' he asked.

'What about?'

'Girls.'

'Girls?'

'Yes, you know. The ones with the bums and tits.'

'Oh – *girls*!'

It was the middle of an Etonian morning and we had all dispersed for Chambers. Masters had retired to Upper School to exchange pleasantries over light refreshments and we were free to eat, drink, rest, play and chat.

'I know some girls who'd like to meet you, Mountjoy,' he continued.

'Why?'

'For the pleasure of your company.'

'How do they know it will be a pleasure?'

'Because they trust my judgement,' he boasted.

Fleet was a person whose company I would not have sought out. He was a sly, cunning, unpopular boy with a pork-pie face and greasy hair. But he knew about girls. We all knew that he knew.

'What sort of girls are they?' I wondered.

'Pretty ones. They're students.'

'Of what?'

'Come and find out.'

I suppose I should have walked away from him right then but my interest was aroused. I was of an age to be desperate for female contact without knowing how to achieve it. My experience of the opposite sex had so far been limited to Davinia and Rosemary Anne, and I had come to accept that there were several gradations of girlhood between implacable hatred and magnificent obsession.

The curiosity factor was a strong one. Unprepossessing as he was, Fleet somehow had the knack of reeling in attractive girlfriends. He had been seen with a bevy of them during the last June the Fourth celebrations. Like most of the other boys, I envied his swaggering confidence and his air of worldliness.

'What harm can it do?' he pressed.

'Let me think it over, Fleet.'

'It could be to your advantage, you know.'

'In what way?'

'You'll see.'

Fleet left it at that. Having baited the hook, he strolled off.

I was in a quandary. Though I was anxious to take counsel, it was impossible for me to raise the matter with Gordy. When you are madly in love with someone's sister – as I was with Rosemary Anne – you cannot have detailed discussions about other girls with her brother. In any case, Gordy's ignorance was far greater than my own. Beside

Fleet, I might be a floundering amateur: compared with Gordy Hollis, however, I was a seasoned voluptuary.

Days of anguished thought ended with a second approach.

'Have you made up your mind yet?'

'I need more time, Fleet.'

'Forget it, then,' he said dismissively.

'Why?'

'Because it had to be tonight or not at all.'

'Tonight!'

'Only day they could all manage.' He heaved a sigh. 'I'll just have to ring them and say it's all off.'

'No, don't do that!' I blurted out.

'Good man, Mountjoy! I knew you wouldn't let me down.'

'I haven't said I'll do it yet,' I stressed, then I thought about the logistics of the exercise. 'Anyway, how can you possibly smuggle some girls into the College?'

'I can't: I smuggle us out.'

'Where to?'

'Windsor. One of the girls has a flat. Ideal for the party.'

'What party?'

'The one they want to throw in your honour.'

'Oh . . .' Misgivings assaulted me from all directions.

'Don't you have the bottle, Mountjoy?'

'It isn't that . . .'

'Then say you'll come,' he insisted.

I considered the matter and then nodded. 'As long as it's safe . . .'

'Leave that side of it to me. Be ready at eight. On the dot.'

It was all arranged. My debut. Too late to turn back.

When I met Fleet that evening, I reeled from the impact of his after-shave. He must have taken a bath in the stuff. Wearing a dirty raincoat and a battered trilby, he looked at once seedy and raffish. He motioned for me to follow and led me quietly down the back stairs. Autumn mist compounded the darkness and gave us ample cover as we sneaked out of the building. Fleet took me on a twisting route that eventually brought us to the wall. It was a matter of seconds before we had climbed over it.

I was excited but still unclear on detail.

'What exactly will I have to do, Fleet?'

'Just play it by ear.'

'How many girls will there be?'

'Five or six. And whatever happens, we go fifty-fifty.'

'Fifty-fifty?'

'I set everything up, remember.'

'I know but – '

'Here's Beryl!'

A Mini approached, flashed its lights at us, then pulled up at the kerb. Fleet bundled me into the back seat then sat in the front beside a small but vivacious young woman in her early twenties.

'Hello, Christopher,' she said, bubbling. 'I'm Beryl.'

'Pleased to meet you.'

'The pleasure's all mine, love!'

Her tone was vulgar but appreciative and I liked her at once. She drove us towards Windsor and chatted amiably about the other girls. Fleet was completely at ease with her and I envied his ability to make her laugh with his small talk. Shyness and inexperience were still keeping me fairly silent.

We reached a pub in the main street and went into the car park.

'I thought we were going to someone's flat,' I observed.

'We are, love,' replied Beryl with a titter. 'Later on. When Tracey's husband goes out.'

'Husband?'

'He doesn't know about our little party.'

As we got out of the car and moved towards the pub, I fell in beside Fleet. 'We can't go in there. we're under age.'

'You and I know that,' he returned. 'They don't.'

As soon as we entered the lounge bar, we were waved over to a table by four teenage girls. From their laughter and high spirits, I could see that they had already had a few drinks. Fleet moved familiarly among them and introduced them to me.

'Jane – Denise – Yvonne – and Liz!'

'Hello,' I said affably.

They gave me a collective giggle and gathered around me when I sat down. Beryl bought some drinks and set a pint of beer down in front of me. I sipped it out of politeness and tried to field some of the questions that were being hurtled at me.

'We've 'eard so much about you, Chris. Is it all true?'

'Do you really live in a dirty great castle?'

'With 'undreds of servants? Butlers, maids and that?'

'Is your father really a millionaire?'

'With a Mediterranean yacht and an 'ouse in the Bahamas?'

'And money to burn?'

Fleet had obviously laid it on with a trowel. I felt like a stately home under seige by a charabanc of shop girls but somehow I did not mind. They were all pert, attractive creatures and I was actually starting to enjoy their company. Whether it was the beer or the warmth of their welcome I do not know, but I felt much more at home with that little gaggle of Windsor teenagers than I had ever done with the well-bred dervishes that Davinia used to inflict on me from her school. These girls were there to have fun *with* me and not at my expense. It was a novel sensation and I liked it.

In telling them all about me, Fleet had not omitted the crucial detail. They knew. Innuendoes and giggles spiced their chatter and they took it in turns to gaze wonderingly at my thighs. For once, I was neither embarrassed nor wearied by it all. Indeed, after a second pint of beer, I was even ready to bask in the adulation.

Beryl slipped out to make a telephone call and returned with a grin of triumph. 'All clear, girls!'

'Over to Tracey's,' ordered Fleet.

Drinks were finished and coats put on then we all poured out of the bar and ambled down the street. The cold night air did not dispel the party atmosphere that we had generated and the laughter continued all the way. The flat was only a few minutes' walk away and was situated above a shoe shop. There was a living room with a kitchen unit in one corner, a bedroom and a bathroom.

The living room was so badly lit that we could hardly see Tracey. Because she was married, I had expected her to be older than the others but she was instead the youngest of them all. Like the rest of them, she wore pungent scent and too much make-up but I was ready to make all sorts of allowances now. Pop music played, warm white wine was handed around and the party went on. The constraints imposed by the pub no longer existed.

Beryl suddenly cackled and looped an arm through mine.

'The rest of you can bugger off 'ome!'

It did not sound like the Joke of the Decade but the girls screamed and hooted and clapped their hands for minutes. Beryl was their natural leader and she revelled in her role.

'Trust you, Beryl Riley!'

'Wait till I tell Tone.'

'Yeah, 'e ought to keep you on a bloody leash.'

'Can't get enough, can you!'

'Leave a bit for me, Ber!'

It was all a bit raucous and uncontrolled but I found myself smiling tolerantly. Three glasses of wine conspired with the beer to release me from all my inhibitions. I could have done with less cigarette smoke and quieter music but I did not complain. We were all having a marvellous time.

Fleet was acting as a kind of stage manager, filling glasses, moving around the girls, keeping the spirit of the party going. I was grateful to him. In a couple of hours, I had taken giant steps towards manhood and I would obviously take a few more before the evening was over. I was in a mood to go along with everything.

'Better not leave it too late,' decided Fleet.

'No. Geoff'll be back at midnight,' noted Tracey.

'Wouldn't 'e 'ave a shock if 'e saw us now?' said Liz.

'Get the show rolling!' demanded Beryl.

'Yes!' I agreed, raising my glass to her.

Fleet took me by the arm and guided me into the bedroom. A small table lamp threw a gentle glow on the bed as I flopped down on it with a laugh. Fleet was calm and businesslike.

'Don't forget, Mountjoy. Fifty-fifty.'

'Which three do you want?' I asked then gave an involuntary yawn.

'Hey! Don't go to sleep on me!' he warned, shaking me. 'Those girls want some action.'

'Send them in!' I said, untroubled by my total lack of experience.

'You've got two flashes, two feels and a full works.'

'A full *what*?'

'Beryl,' he explained. 'She wants to go the whole hog. As usual. Oh, and keep a bit in reserve for Tracey. She gets a freebie for loaning us the flat.'

'A freebie!'

'All the others have paid. Three quid for a flash, five for a feel and ten for the whole bit. That's thirteen quid each for us.'

I was instantly sober and on my feet. Fun and frolic was one thing but I drew the line at sordid commercial transaction. Instead of being my friend, Fleet was trying to be my pimp.

I was angry with him and even angrier with myself.

'Give them their money back. I'm leaving.'

'You can't!' he pleaded. 'They'll tear us to pieces if you don't give them what they want. I've been building them up to this all week, Mountjoy. They demand satisfaction.'

'Then *you* give it to them!'

'I can't!' he wailed. 'They want King Kong not Mr Average.'

'I'll speak to them,' I said confidently. 'They'll understand.'

'Don't go in there!'

Brushing aside his protests, I opened the door to face the partygoers who set up a lewd cheer. Girls who had seemed nice, normal and fairly controlled in the pub now had a mad, inflamed look about them.

'Ladies, there has been a slight misunderstanding . . . '

'Get 'em off!' yelled Beryl.

'Owing to circumstances beyond my control, I have to leave now . . . '

'Over my dead body!' asserted Tracey.

'And my live one!' added Beryl.

'Unfortunately, I have a prior engagement,' I said. 'So if you will all kindly excuse me, I will just – '

I got no further. Mutiny stirred. It soon found a leader.

'*I* have a prior bloody engagement as well!' howled Beryl, waving her fist like a professional rabble-rouser. 'With you.'

'Some other time,' I suggested. 'When I can fit it in.'

'You'll fit it in right now!'

And before I could stop her, she threw herself at me and dragged me back into the bedroom. As she kicked the door closed behind her, the others clapped and shouted encouragement. They were not partygoers any longer but rampant females forming a queue for me.

'This is what I want!' explained Beryl, pushing me to the bed with forthright lust. 'No more teasing.'

'But I wasn't teasing you. In fact – '

The rest of my sentence was spoken into a large, moist mouth. Beryl started the proceedings with a wet, slobbery kiss that left me feeling as if I had just taken a cold shower. She sat up, took hold of her sweater and pulled it off completely. Her bra soon followed the sweater to the floor and two small, pink, conicle breasts came into view. Erect nipples twitched at me by way of enticement.

'Do my tits!' she ordered.

'They look as if they're already done, Beryl.'

'Get busy!'

Still recovering from the slobbery kiss, my mouth now found itself invaded by one of the breasts. She pressed and rotated it at me so much that I felt as if I was suffocating. My teeth closed involuntarily.

She withdrew at once with a screech of pain.

'Is it really *that* big?' called Tracey from outside.

It was no time for gentlemanly behaviour. Grabbing Beryl, I opened the door and thrust her into the middle of her friends then I slammed the door shut, put a chair underneath the handle to hold the first rush. Opening the window, I put a leg over the sill and explored fresh air.

As the door burst under a concerted charge, I jumped out.

The soles of my feet burned as I hit the pavement and I was pitched backwards but there seemed to be no serious damage. With concerted abuse coming at me from the open window, I picked myself up and sprinted off down the street.

Fleet was left behind to suffer the consequences.

When the Christmas holidays came, Mountjoy Manor welcomed me back as if I had never been away and then treated me as if I were not there. The family was still largely invisible – even on Christmas Day – and the only person with whom I spent any length of time was Nanny Groat. We would sit huddled over the stove in her woodshed and talk about those in peril on the sea.

During one of these nautical chats, I caught a glimpse through the window of a Grenadier Guard marching along the other side of the privet hedge. His busby bounced up and down as he moved and added extra height that was almost intimidating. I was very surprised when Nanny Groat leapt to her feet and touched her cap in deference. She was, after all, effectively a member of the Senior Service.

'Why did you do that, Nanny?'

'I always show respect to Lady Mountjoy.'

'That was *mother*!'

'She's bought herself a new wig.'

When the Grenadier Guard emerged from behind the hedge, it was indeed mother. Seeing me through the window, she waved with a gloved hand before heading for the Off Licence she had recently had built near the gatehouse.

Pleasant as it was to see Nanny again and to lapse back into my old part as her cabin boy, I soon began to miss company of my own age. I was delighted, therefore, when Gordy rang to invite me to Kenilworth for the New Year. Having sent a note to father asking for permission to go, I received a Bon Voyage card signed for him by an underling with an italic pen. Next day I caught a train for leafy Warwickshire.

Rosemary Anne kissed me on the cheek by way of a welcome.

'Lovely to see you again, Christopher!'

'Thanks. Have a good Christmas?'

'Smashing. You?'

'Bit quiet.'

'We'll soon make up for that.'

She had grown and matured but she was essentially the girl I had fallen in love with on my first visit. There was the same zest, the same sense of fun, the same passion for riding and the same tomboy heartiness. I learned that I was not the only guest. Rosemary Anne had invited a schoolfriend for the New Year as well.

Carlotta Nashe was a rather big, slovenly girl who was running to fat. Subdued, watchful and polite, she had large brown eyes set wide apart in a nondescript face. Like Rosemary Anne, she was a keen horsewoman and went out for a hack every day. Gordy and I watched the two of them one morning.

'Don't you think she's wonderful, Christopher?'

'Yes!' I agreed, entranced by his sister.

'She's so bright and intelligent!'

'I know.'

'Such a sincere person.'

'She's got everything!' I confirmed.

'Yes. I'm so glad she came to stay with us.'

Gordy was talking about the plump and ponderous Carlotta Nashe. And he was in love. It was a new departure for him and he was justifiably bewildered. He sought my advice.

'Christopher . . . '

'Yes?'

'Do you think that Carlotta likes me?'

'Everybody likes you, Gordy.'

'Yes, but does *she*?'

'Of course.'

'Have you actually heard her say so?' he interrogated.

'Not in so many words. But she'd be mad not to like you.'

He gazed fondly after her. 'I want her to be my wife.'

'Hold on, old chap! You've only just met the girl!'

'It doesn't matter. I *know*.'

'Well, I shouldn't mention the fact to her,' I cautioned. 'Something tells me that Carlotta is not ready to talk about marriage just yet.'

'Oh, I won't say a thing, Christopher. I'm far too shy.' He gave me a sheepish grin. 'Be honest, though. Don't you think that she and I would make a perfect couple?'

'Yes, yes!' I lied with a conviction born of friendship.

Love is indeed blind. When Gordy looked at Carlotta Nashe, he did not notice that she was almost a foot taller than him and that she tipped the scales at a couple of stone heavier. There was something else he had not seen. Carlotta might appear subdued but those large brown eyes of her spoke of fire and passion. Sexually, she was well above Gordy's fighting weight. He would not survive one round.

'I don't suppose . . . '

'Go on,' I urged.

'I don't suppose you'd speak to her for me?'

'What do you want me to say?'

'Just . . . sound her out, Christopher.'

'What about?'

'Everything. Her background. Her likes and dislikes. Her hopes. Her ambitions. What size shoes she wears. Everything!' The sheepish grin returned. 'And sound her out about me. Tactfully.'

'I'll do my best, Gordy.'

'Thanks! I'll do the same for you one day.'

Without realizing it, he had been doing just that for years because I had pumped him relentlessly about Rosemary Anne. While I had kept my love a secret throughout all that time, however, Gordy was confessing his infatuation within days of the first symptoms.

I managed some time alone with Carlotta that afternoon. Sounding her out did not prove an easy task. I tried to sound casual.

'Where do you come from, Carlotta?'

'Same place as Rosemary Anne. Cheltenham Ladies' College.'

'But where do you live?'

'Cheltenham.'

'Is there anything you really like?'

'Cheltenham.'

'What about dislikes?'

'Cheltenham Ladies' College.'

'Hopes?'

'To go on living in Cheltenham.'

'Ambitions?'

'To leave Cheltenham Ladies' College.'

She was playing with me. We went around in circles for another ten minutes before I gave up. The brown eyes twinkled mischievously.

'By the way, I take size six in shoes.'

'Oh.'

'And I think Gordy is a bit of a joke.'

'He's a splendid chap!' I defended.

'Yes, I know. I like him. He makes me laugh.'

There was no point in going any further. I did not want to hear anything else that I could not possibly tell my best friend. As I tried to disengage myself, however, Carlotta gave me a cool stare and cut through my excuses with a question that was chilling in its accuracy and directness.

'How long have you had a crush on Rosemary Anne?'

'I, er . . . well . . . '

'It's alright. *She* doesn't know anything about it.'

'Then how did . . . ?'

'I have a nose for these things,' she said arily, 'for what it's worth, Rosemary Anne likes you a lot.'

It was worth everything. I cherished that piece of information as if it were a lucky charm and kept taking it out to examine it. In trying to help Gordy, I had instead found out something to my own advantage. It was ironic.

When Gordy cross-examined me, I had to edit my findings.

'She's fond of you,' I assured him.

'Is that the truth, Christopher?'

'She finds you witty and amusing.'

'But I'm too tongue-tied to say anything to her.'

'Carlotta makes allowances for that.'

'Marvellous!' he said with an inane laugh. 'What about everything else? Background, likes, dislikes, hopes, ambitions?'

I reduced it all to its essence. 'Size six.'

Gordy was thrilled by the intelligence. His face beamed.

New Year's Eve was a revelation. Accustomed to spending it alone in my room at Mountjoy Manor, I was amazed to see that some people made a real fuss of the event. Mr and Mrs Hollis had a small party for close friends. There was food, drink, fun, games, dancing and a wonderful family atmosphere. As midnight approached, we all gathered around the television to watch the Hogmanay celebrations. I took care to get next to Rosemary Anne, who looked lovely in a red party dress. Gordy, I saw, had positioned himself near Carlotta.

As the chimes boomed out, we linked hands and sang Auld Lang Syne before turning to each other to put a more personal signature on the New Year. Rosemary Anne kissed me full on the lips then gave a hearty laugh. Enraptured as I was, I found time to look across at Gordy. As he lunged inexpertly at Carlotta, she took his head between her hands and gave him a token peck on the forehead. He was overjoyed.

Kisses were now traded at random and Carlotta worked her way around to me. Putting a hand under my chin, she touched my lips very softly with hers then stared deep into my eyes. I was totally confused. Though I loved Rosemary Anne to distraction, it was Carlotta's kiss that really aroused me.

I lay in bed for hours trying to work it all out.

Now an accomplished rider, I began the next day with half an hour in the saddle. Rosemary Anne and Carlotta stood at the gate of the paddock and watched me. They were talking and laughing and it was obvious that I was the subject of their conversation. When I took the horse back to the stable to feed and untack it, Carlotta joined me.

'Tonight, Christopher.'

'What?'

'Rosemary Anne will see you tonight.'

'Where?'

'Up there,' she said, pointing to the hay-loft. 'At midnight.'

'But what for, Carlotta?'

'Even you don't have to be told that, surely?' she teased.

'Why hasn't Rosemary Anne asked me herself?'

'You've still got a lot to learn,' she noted.

'Midnight!' I promised. 'I'll be there!'

'Be on time. A girl doesn't like to be kept waiting.'

She went out and left me vibrating with expectation.

Over luncheon and again over tea, I kept a close watch on Rosemary Anne but she gave me no hidden signals. Our nocturnal tryst had been arranged through a third party and she was pretending that she knew nothing about it. She was saving her signals for the hay-loft.

Gordy was a problem. As we lay in our beds in the darkness of his room that night, he burbled on about Carlotta for what seemed like hours. It was nearly midnight when he finally went off to meet his beloved in his dreams. I moved swiftly and quietly. When I got to the bathroom, I took out the sweater and the jeans I had concealed in the airing cupboard and slipped them on over my pyjamas. Sneaking out to the verandah at the back of the house, I stepped into a pair of gumboots and pulled on my anorak.

It was cold and dark outside but I was not troubled by that. To reach Rosemary Anne for an assignation, I would have braved anything. When I reached the stable, I heard the horse stir in its loose box but I could make nothing out in the gloom. I stood there for several minutes but nothing happened. It slowly began to dawn on me that I was the victim of a cruel schoolgirl joke. Rosemary Anne was not coming out to the stable at all.

'Christopher!' came a low hiss from above.

'Where are you, Rosemary Anne?' I whispered.

'Up here.' There was a rustling sound. 'In the straw.'

I stumbled around the stable until I felt the ladder then I went up its rungs at speed. The rustling was only feet away from me now. I reached out a hand and touched Rosemary Anne's shoulder. She took charge of proceedings from that point on.

Grabbing me by the wrist, she pulled me on top of her and fixed her mouth to mine. Her kisses were long, desperate and searching. The biting cold of a winter's night soon became the sensual heat of a tropical paradise as we bucked and twisted and flailed about.

When she put my hand up under her sweater so that I could feel her bare breast, I twanged like a tuning fork.

Seeing her naked that time had aroused me, but this was a far more powerful source of wonder and excitement. As I kneaded her breast softly with my fingers, I felt as if I was about to explode with joy.

Rosemary Anne had her legs wide apart and she kept pressing down rhythmically on my buttocks with her palms. Her breathing hardened, her writhing increased to a frenzy and her passion soared like a space rocket until she suddenly thrust up her loins at me and dug her nails into my flesh.

Then she let out a moan of such volume and intensity that it frightened the horse and terrified me. When it was all over, she lay in the darkness and panted. I rolled off her.

'Rosemary Anne,' I whispered. 'Are you alright?'

'Fine!' said a different voice.

'Carlotta!'

'That was fantastic!' she gasped.

'But I thought it was Rosemary Anne!' I protested.

'That's okay,' she replied. 'I pretended it was Robert Redford.'

'You got me here under false pretences.'

'I wanted you so I had you. What's false about that?'

'It's so unfair, Carlotta!'

'Why?'

'If I'd known it was you, I wouldn't have come up here.'

'But it was me,' she argued. 'And you *did* come up. Hard.'

'This is terrible! You deceived Rosemary Anne.'

'So did you. Shall I tell her about it?'

'No!' I exclaimed.

'Shall I tell her that you seduced me?' she teased.

'It was the other way around. You're wicked, Carlotta.'

'I know,' she said with a giggle. 'That's why you fancied me.'

'I do not fancy you.'

'Okay. *You* may not but you're body certainly does. Or was that a bicycle pump you had in your trouser pocket?'

'Please!' I complained, blushing deeply.

She nuzzled up to me. 'I'm ready again. I want to go off.'

'Good. I'll walk back up to the house with you.'

'Go off up here, stupid!' she corrected. 'Just like now.'

'Think of the horse.'

'Come on top of me,' she whispered.

'No.'

'You like it when I do this, don't you?' she said, flicking her tongue inside my ear.

'No.'

'And you like it when I do that, don't you?' she added, stroking the inside of my thigh until it became a forest fire.

'No,' I denied through clenched teeth.

'And I know you just love *these*!'

She put both my hands up under her sweater and on to her breasts. The twang of the tuning fork was more audible this time. Carlotta laughed and hauled me on top of her.

'Let's do it again!' she commanded.

And I have to admit that we did.

Chapter Five: EXIT FROM ETON

The battle of Waterloo was won on the playing fields of Eton and many hearts have been lost at the same venue. Whenever I turned out for the rugby team, I became acutely aware of my personal contribution to this tradition of blighted romance. Saucer-eyed youths would watch me from all sides and applaud generously if I so much as caught the ball. Since I played on the wing and was frequently tackled into touch, I had to get used to being helped up by dozens of willing hands.

It is disturbing to be the object of so much unrequited love but you learn to take it in your stride and to concentrate on the game. During our annual battle of Waterloo with Harrow one afternoon, I encountered a new variation on this old problem. I was being watched. Not only by my faithful band of torch-bearers. Not only by the delirious Etonian supporters who roared us on to victory. And not only by the glum and resentful visiting spectators.

I was under surveillance by an alien presence.

As we left the field in triumph, Gordy ran over to congratulate me, throwing his scarf around my neck and pounding me unmercifully on the back.

'Well done, Christopher! Great game!'

'I say, Gordy, can you *see* anybody?'

'Hundreds of people.'

'Can you see anybody who is looking at *me*?'

'Everybody is, you silly chump! You just scored the winning try.'

'Did I?' It must have happened when I had switched over

to automatic pilot. 'Gordy, are you *sure* there's nobody spying on me?'

'You've got a persecution complex,' he said, falling back on one of our favourite jokes. 'When they scrum down, you think they're all talking about you.'

'I can just *feel* a pair of eyes on me,' I insisted.

'Figment of your imagination, old chap.'

But it was not. From that day on, it got steadily worse.

I would be coming down the steps of College Chapel or crossing the worn cobbles of School Yard or strolling beside the river or doing any one of a dozen other things, when it would happen. That prickly sensation. The awareness that I had company. It was eerie.

The invigilation continued for weeks before I got my first clue as to the identity of my shadow. We were out for a training run in a light drizzle when I spotted something in the distance. It was a pair of binoculars peeping around the trunk of an oak tree and I knew that they were focused on me. I stopped dead in my tracks. The binoculars vanished at once and then a squat female figure emerged and waddled off at speed. Her umbrella obscured her from me but I had at least learned one thing.

My phantom follower was a middle-aged woman.

Eton had changed Gordy Hollis. The cherubic face of his first year had thinned and lengthened now and he had shed that does-your-mother-know-you're-out look that had made him so vulnerable in the past. What struck you about him most was his air of joyful commitment. There was a tell-tale glow about him that told you he must either end up as a musician or a parish priest.

Our housemaster was guiding him towards the former.

'Dexter thinks I could win a music scholarship.'

'You could fiddle your way into anywhere,' I encouraged.

'He also went on about the birds and the bees.'

'Oh. I don't like the sound of that.'

'Neither did I the way that Dexter explained it.'

'What do you mean, Gordy?'

'According to him, it all boils down to this: every time a woman is stung by a bee, she lays a canary egg.'

'I think you may have misunderstood him.'

'I hope so, Christopher!' he said with feeling. 'It got really embarrassing in there. He even asked me how far I'd gone.'

'Gone?'

'With a girl.'

'What did you say?'

'That I'd been to Benidorm with Rosemary Anne.'

'I don't think that's what he meant,' I suggested.

'It wasn't. But I couldn't tell him the truth, could I?'

'What truth?'

'About Carlotta and me.'

'Something *happened* between you two?'

'Of course. You were there. New Year's Eve.'

'And?'

'Carlotta kissed me on the forehead. I couldn't tell Dexter about *that* now, could I? He'd think I was a sex maniac.' A faraway look came into his eye. 'Besides, I owe it to Carlotta to keep our little secret. You wouldn't tell if it had happened to you, would you?'

'No, Gordy,' I promised, '*I* wouldn't say anything about Carlotta.'

And so I didn't. His fantasies could be preserved. Gordy was far too young to be told about the antics in the hay-loft. No matter how long he lived, Gordy would always be too young to know about that.

We were standing outside the housemaster's study. Gordy had just come from his interview and I was waiting to go in for mine. Dexter liked to have a session with each of his senior boys some time in that year. He called the interview his Go Forward chat and it was designed to point us in the right direction. If Gordy's experience was anything to judge by, the Go Forward chat was much more likely to set you back. I was dreading my turn.

Gordy had been ruminating quietly. He spoke wistfully.

'They take it seriously at Cheltenham Ladies' College.'
'What?'
'Sex.'
'How do you know?'
'Rosemary Anne told me. It's on the syllabus.'
'Sex education lessons?'
'They do it with goats.'

Before he could elaborate on this startling news, the door opened and Fleet came out of the study. His sneer changed to a scowl when he saw me. He had still not forgiven me for leaving him to face the merry wives of Windsor and their friends.

'Good luck, Christopher!'

'Thanks, Gordy. I may need it.'

I knocked on the door, entered and got a sinister leer from Dexter.

'Take a seat, Mountjoy.'

'Thank you, sir,' I said, sitting in front of the desk.

'I'm sure you know why you're here,' he began.

'Yes, sir.'

'Forward planning. Choosing the right road. Following the correct signpost. Avoiding cul-de-sacs.' He washed his hands in the air. 'Have you thought about your future at all?'

'I want to travel, sir.'

'As a career?' He sounded dubious.

'I'm not certain yet.'

'I would have thought a degree was your first port of call.'

'But I'm no scholar, sir.'

'It's true that you have not exactly distinguished yourself in the academic sphere but with a little application and a following wind, you should be able to scrape a congratulatory Third at one of the dingier Polytechnics.'

'I think I'd rather travel, sir. Broaden the mind.'

'A fallacy, in my view. I've never met any set of human beings more consistently narrow-minded than travel agents.' He set about his moustache as if he were plucking a turkey. 'However, if you wish to travel in order to go to a university abroad, that is quite another matter. I could give my blessing to that. Paris, say. Or Heidelberg. Even America. Yes, your sporting prowess would be an asset there.'

'I *have* to travel, sir,' I explained patiently. 'When I've seen the world, I can decide what to do with my life.'

'Seeing the world is another overrated concept,' he argued. 'I always advise against it. The expense is never worth it and you greatly increase the range of diseases you might catch. I had an uncle who died in Calcutta because he wanted to "see the world". What do you say to that, Mountjoy?'

I said that I would take his advice and consider a university course. If I held out for what I wanted to do, I might be there for a week. It was better to take the line of least resistance.

'That brings me to the facts of life . . . '

'Are they really necessary, sir?' I asked, trying to head him off.

'Of course. How else would we be here?'

'I meant, is it necessary for you to tell me about them?'

'Would *you* rather tell *me*?'

'No!'

'Then pay attention. I would hate any boy from this house to be sent out into the world ignorant of the reproductive process.'

I braced myself just in time. Relying heavily on metaphor and allusion, he talked about the facts of life for ten minutes or more without giving me a single piece of hard information. It was obvious that my housemaster knew as little about the subject as I did. He seemed to think that sexual intercourse was like brass rubbing: you did as thorough a job as you could and hoped you had made a good impression.

He came to the end of his lecture and regarded me sternly.

'Have you ever had any, Mountjoy?'

'Any what, sir?'

'Personal experience of what I have just described.'.

'Oh yes,' I said blithely.

'Indeed!'

'We have several monumental brasses at Mountjoy Manor.'

'Sacrilege!'

'I've had a go at most of them over the years.'

'You should be ashamed of yourself!' he said in shocked tones. 'Self-abuse can lead to blindness. Not to mention the damage you might have done to the monumental brasses!' He took some time to recover his calm then stared over at me. 'Any questions?'

'What's the difference between sex and reproduction, sir?'

'The former is something you enjoy: and the latter is something you regret for the rest of your life.' His eye fell on the framed photograph of his wife and he reached out to touch it with his fingers, pulling them back at once as if they had been bitten. 'That is the end of the interview, Mountjoy.'

'Thank you, sir.'

'It only remains for me to invite you to tea tomorrow.'

'Tea, sir?'

'With Mrs Dexter and myself.'

'Oh. I see.'

'We shall expect you at four.' He closed the blue eye and glared at me with the green one. 'I need hardly say that I want no mention in front of my wife of your activities with the monumental brasses.'

'Not a word, sir. Besides, I haven't done it for ages.'

'Remorse?'

'No, sir. To be honest, I found it rather painful.'

He stood up and escorted me to the door. As I was about to leave, I saw something I had not noticed before. On a table in the far corner was a pair of binoculars.

'Do those belong to you, sir?' I asked.

'Yes. My wife has been borrowing them.'

'Why?'

'Who knows?' he said evasively. 'Perhaps Mrs Dexter has taken up aircraft-spotting. We are in the flight-path to Heathrow, after all.' He ushered me out. 'Tomorrow at four, Mountjoy.'

'I'll be there, sir.'

Polly Dexter had been at Eton College so long that she was taken for granted. Like a gargoyle, she was an accepted feature of a sacred structure. With the buoyant cruelty which distinguishes the young from its elders, we called her Pretty Polly, a nickname that was both an ironic comment on her legendary ugliness and a subtle joke on her uncanny likeness – in profile, wearing a fur coat – to a parrot.

Pretty Polly was seen but not heard. She had the grim, vindictive, soured look of a woman who has made one ghastly mistake and who is doomed to spend the rest of her life atoning for it.

Dexter was that mistake.

'Do come on in, Mountjoy!' he said with laboured joviality.

'Thank you, sir.'

'You've met Mrs Dexter, haven't you?'

'Hello, Mrs Dexter.'

'I'll fetch the tea,' she grunted.

'Very kind of you to invite me.'

'And the cake.'

Their living room was like a badly-designed set for a play by Galsworthy. It had a dated awfulness to it and I have known bus shelters with a more homely feel. I sat on an undulating sofa beside Dexter and watched his wife bring in a tray.

She served tea in stony silence. Looking at this weird, embittered, unfeminine creature with her hair swept venomously back and held tight in a bun, I could not believe that she was the person who had trailed me so steadfastly. Mrs Dexter was ignoring me.

Her husband munched a piece of cake and launched into a

speech about the virtues of Eton in the pre-war period. When he finished there was an awesome hush and I felt obliged to say something.

'I want to ask you something, sir.'

'Ask away, Mountjoy.'

'It arose out of our chat yesterday . . .'

He went on the defensive. 'Not about brasses, is it?'

'No, sir. It's about Calcutta.'

'Calcutta?'

'That uncle of yours who wanted to see the world.'

'Ah yes! Poor Uncle Stanley!'

'What exactly did he die of out there?'

'Lead poisoning,' replied Dexter. 'He shot himself six times. And if that doesn't put you off the idea of travel, nothing will!'

We finished our tea and then my housemaster put everything on the tray and took it out into the kitchen. I could hear him running water to do the washing up and so I turned to his wife.

'Would your husband like some help. Mrs Dexter?'

'No.'

'I'd be glad to lend a hand.'

'No.'

'Do you have many boys to tea here?'

'No.'

'Then I'm honoured. Thank you. I've enjoyed it.'

There was another long silence then I heard a strange noise. It sounded at first like the squeaking of a mouse, then it became the tearing of a piece of sandpaper, then it became the splintering of a plank of wood. Finally, it swelled into a violent crescendo that was the melting of an iceberg. It was only when the last crack had resounded that I realized what had happened.

Pretty Polly had smiled at me.

Easter took me back to Mountjoy Manor which had changed very little. It was a week before anyone noticed that I had come home. Father was involved in the takeover of an

Italian company and spaghetti was served with every meal, regardless of its suitability. Mother was preoccupied with the alterations – having tired of the bar she had had built in her bedroom, she was now having a bedroom built in the lounge bar – and with gracing every cocktail party within fifty miles. Barnaby was entrenched in the Civil Service and engaged in a campaign to persuade his young wife to let him do everything in triplicate. And Davinia was continuing to break men's hearts as if she were cracking eggs for some monster omelette.

Nanny Groat, of course, was still Nanny Groat.

'Well, what do you think, matey?'

'Wonderful!'

'You haven't recognized them, have you?'

'Daffodils.' They were there in Wordsworthian profusion. 'I know a daffodil when I see one, Nanny.'

'But you don't know a naval bleeding battle!'

'Battle?' I stared blankly at the flowerbed.

'I've planted them in the exact formation Nelson's ships took during the attack on the filthy French in Aboukir Bay. See now, you young devil? Each daff is a sail. White for England, yellow for the Frogs.' She chewed her clay pipe in disgust. 'What the hell do they learn you at that bleeding school? Didn't you realize you were looking at the Battle of the Nile?'

Only Nanny could combine horticulture with heroism on the high seas. In time, no doubt, she would go on to produce a briar rose that could sing shanties.

The highlight of the holidays was Gordy's visit to Mountjoy Manor. I quizzed him carefully about Rosemary Anne and pined inwardly for her. He was still worshipping Carlotta Nashe from afar. That kiss on the forehead had been his sexual baptism.

'I know that she can never be mine!' he sighed.

'Why?'

'Because she's so pure and untouchable.'

'*Carlotta*?'

'She's the type of girl who will go to her grave undefiled.'

Without saying so, I agreed with him. Her funeral might be the one occasion when she would draw the line at misbehaviour. It would be a restful conclusion to what I suspected would be a lifetime of unstinting service to the male sex.

'You do like Carlotta, don't you?'

'Of course, Gordy.'

'I do so want you to get on together.'

'We did. I mean – we do.'

'I'd hate there to be any friction between you.'

'No comment.'

Gordy's innocence was touching. He was always ready to think well of people and place the kindest construction on their actions. I expected that even he would rumble Davinia – as I now had, to my eternal disgust – but he did not. When a succession of lusty young men came calling for her in fast cars, he decided she had taken up rally driving. The true nature of her hobby was obscured from him.

He came to me in a puzzled mood one morning.

'I didn't know that Davinia was religious.'

'Neither did I, Gordy,' I confessed.

'I've just come from that chapel with all the books.'

'That's the library.'

'I popped in for something to read and there was Davinia. I didn't actually see her because she was behind that enormous sofa. Kneeling down, obviously. Praying.'

'How do you know that?'

'Because I heard the prayer quite clearly. "Oh God! I'm coming!' she said. Then God answered: "So am I!" It was rather moving.'

Blessed are the pure in mind for they shall see nothing.

June the Fourth at Eton College is no ordinary day in the calendar. Ostensibly, it is a celebration of the birthday of mad old George III who used to talk to the trees in nearby Windsor Castle but it is also an occasion for speeches, songs, picnics, performances, processions on the river, languid cricket, luxurious idleness, dressing up, showing off and remembering above all that you are English. The kind of day, in short, when elitism starts to make sense at last.

It was not jolly boating weather. Instead of the recommended hay harvest breeze, there was the merest whisper of wind beneath an overcast sky. The day began with Chapel and then the headmaster called Absence – a list of the present – from the steps outside. We were all there. Young, old, bright, stupid, smart, unkempt, alert and bored. Doting families lurked in their finery to hear the ring of their son's name. Mildewed with age and speckled with bird droppings, the Founder's Statue listened impassively.

In the middle of all those people, I felt lonely. Every other boy seemed to have family or friends there. I longed to have Mountjoys near me for moral support. Father reminiscing about his days at Eton. Mother lying on a rug beneath a willow tree and toying with a bottle of Moet and Chandon. Barnaby describing the tiger-skin waistcoat he wore as a member of Pop. Even Davinia. No, perhaps not. Blood is thicker than water but it should not be spilled on June the Fourth.

Isolated and unprotected, I had been forced to accept an invitation to tea with the Dexters, man and parrot. Even when the weather brightened, their invitation hung over me like a black cloud. They seemed to be following me around. Pretty Polly had raided what must have been her grandmother's wardrobe to dig out a long, swishing dress in cream-coloured lace. From beneath the brim of her straw hat, she kept shooting little smiles at me and even raised her hand to wiggle her fingers at me. It was all very disconcerting.

Afternoon came and I managed to shake them off. I had a blissful hour watching the cricket before I was interrupted. Dexter came up behind me and startled me with his sing-song announcement.

'We're ready for you-oo-oo-oo!'

'Oh. Hello, sir.'

'Are you ready for us, Mountjoy?'

'I suppose so, sir.'

'Then walk back to our lodgings.'

'Lodgings?'

'For tea.'

'Ah, yes.'

'I'll go on ahead,' he insisted. 'Don't keep us waiting, will you? Mrs Dexter has been looking forward to this for a long time.'

The sinister thing about him was that he was no longer sinister.

I wondered why he went striding off instead of accompanying me. And why tea in his dreary lodgings? I had hoped for a Fortnum and Mason's hamper by the river or a full spread in the refreshment marquee. Everybody else was having a glorious Fourth of June. While they enjoyed sunshine and celebration, I would be stuck in a Galsworthy play with a frustrated academic and his brass rubbing.

I set off with profound misgivings. As I came around the angle of a tent, I saw the lodgings in the distance and was just in time to glimpse Dexter going in through the side door. I dragged my feet but they eventually got me to the building.

Pretty Polly was waiting for me.

'Do step right in, Christopher!'

The grim basilisk now had a girlish gaiety. She drew me into the living room and I sniffed the air. Miss Dior. Gallons of it.

'I want this to be a memorable occasion for all of us,' she said.

'Why? What are we going to eat?'

She laughed tinnily. 'You'll see.'

'Er, where is Mr Dexter?'

'Not here.'

'But I just saw him come in.'

'He had to go out again.'

'Won't he be joining us?'

'Later,' she purred. 'But he wanted you to know that he gives his approval to whatever we may do while . . . he's not here. Quentin understands. I've explained why it has to be you.'

'Good.'

'I want you to let yourself go, Christopher.'

'In what way, Mrs Dexter?'

'*Every* way . . . and the name is Polly.'

'That's pretty.'

Alarm bells rang. I studied her carefully and tried to establish why her dress had changed shape. She took my perusal as evidence of desire. Removing her hat with a sweeping gesture, she put a hand on her flabby hip.

'You like what you see?'

'Yes,' I lied, 'I've always admired this room.'

'I like what I see, Christopher,' she said, baring large dentures at me. 'Do you notice what is different?'

'Yes, Mrs Dexter.'

'Polly,' she corrected.

'Polly.' I pointed to the windows. 'You've got new curtains.'

'Don't you notice anything different about *me*?'

She took a few steps towards me and her dress altered its shape once more. My mouth went dry as I realized why. Pretty Polly was wearing nothing whatsoever underneath the garment. Released from their moorings, her breasts, buttocks and rolls of fat were swilling around all over the place. I backed away involuntarily.

'I watched you for months through the binoculars,' she admitted. 'I simply had to meet you. You're the one person who can bring me to full womanhood.'

'What about your husband?'

'Quentin and I have never really been happy together. He always seems to rub me up the wrong way.' She took hold of my hand. 'But you can alter that, Christopher. You can save our marriage.'

Hypnotised by her dentured smile and anaesthised by her Miss Dior, I made no protest as she led me off to the bedroom. It was only when I saw the bed itself with Dexter's striped pyjamas poking out from beneath the pillow that I came out of my daze.

'What are we doing in here?'

'Submitting to our uncontrollable urges.'

'I think it might be safer if we went back to Mr Dexter, Mrs Dexter. I mean – this is your bedroom!'

'No, Christopher. With you here, it is *ours*!'

She plucked at her bun and long, thin tresses cascaded down to her shoulders. I made a move to the door but she got there first, putting her back against it and laughing in provocation. There was a squeaking noise from behind me.

'What was that?' I asked, turning to look.

'Nothing.'

'But I distinctly heard a – '

'Take me, Christopher!' she bayed.

'Where to?'

'Take me! On the bed! NOW!!!!'

Her dress suddenly fell to the floor and she was naked. Her pink, urgent body featured pendulous breasts, massive thighs and a belly button like the mouth of a miniature Vesuvius. Mobilized by passion, her flesh began to tremble invitingly. It was all too much for me. My mind was telling me to run but my body was giving me the opposite advice. A passable imitation of a fork-lift truck was going on inside my trousers. Pretty Polly noticed.

'He wants me!' she yelled. 'My stallion!'

'Can't we discuss this over a cup of tea?' I suggested.

'I must have it now!'

'Shall I go and put the kettle on?'

'I want you, Christopher!' She pointed to the fork-lift truck. 'I want *that*. All of it!'

She dropped heavily to her knees in front of me and clutched at my trousers. When she yanked them down with my jockey shorts, Great Aunt Lucy popped out to see what all the fuss was about.

Pretty Polly gave a sigh of joy and her whole body shook like a huge, lustful, conglomerate, raspberry jelly.

After thirty starving years, her meal was being served.

Without pausing to say grace, she opened her mouth in a cry of jubilation and moved in for the first bite of ecstasy. Simultaneously, three things happened. Her teeth made contact. Dexter came out of the wardrobe like a Jack-in-the-Box to shout encouragement from the touchline. And the window cleaner appeared at the top of his ladder.

Agony. Voyeurism. Threat of publicity.

I put the fork-lift truck into reverse at once. There was a loud sucking noise and Pretty Polly's dentures came out completely. For one blood-curdling moment, both upper and lower set remained locked on to me before giving me a forlorn smile and dropping to the carpet.

Pretty Polly gulped. Dexter gasped. The window cleaner gaped.

I did all three and made for the door as best I could.

Pursuit was immediate and vengeful.

June the Fourth at Eton College. An unforgettable day. It will certainly never be forgotten by that cluster of visiting ancientry who were gathered around the Provost to hear him talk about the importance of maintaining standards. Eton, he was telling them, was not simply a place. It was an embodiment of all that made England what it was. A symbol. A treasury. An inspiration. An example of unparalleled excellence.

In short, Eton was unique.

What they saw by way of illustration will never be seen again. With his trousers around his ankles, a pale-faced Etonian was hopping along like a demented kangaroo and being chased by a naked, toothless woman, a housemaster in the final stages of frenzy, and a window cleaner with an interest in the wilder aspects of human behaviour.

Our score was two heart attacks, a hernia and a dead faint.

Standing amid the stricken ancientry, the Provost was not amused. Since I was leading the others astray, he singled me out for blame.

'Catch that marsupial!' he roared. 'And bring him to me!'

I lengthened my bounce and headed for home.

Chapter Six: GETTING IN

It was less than a week before I was granted an audience and I was very grateful. There must be sons who have to wait much longer than that to speak to their fathers. I was handed on like a baton from one secretary to another until I finally got into his lair. Father was behind his desk, poring over a chart that showed him how he could ruin five of his business rivals in one easy *coup.* As he seemed to be unaware of my presence, I tapped on the desk with my knuckles. Purely by reflex, he opened a drawer. When he saw that there was nobody in there, he looked up.

'Who might you be, sir?'

'Christopher.'

'Christopher?' It was some time since we had last met.

'Your younger son.'

'I knew the name was familiar.'

'How are you, father?'

'Much better since the pound rallied against the dollar.'

'You're looking well.'

'It's a knack I have,' he said, tossing his mane. 'By the way, I must apologize for having to cancel yesterday's appointment with you. I had to go and try out a new golf club I'd just bought.'

'What was the club? A wood? An iron?'

'Wentworth.'

It was time to get down to cases. 'Have you, er . . . have you had any letters this week, father?'

'I have an enormous mailbag every morning. As a rule, it contains some correspondence for me.'

'Have you had one from Eton, by any chance?'

'A mailbag?'

'A letter.'

'Possibly. I never inspect postmarks.'

'It was from my headmaster.' I swallowed hard. 'About me.'

'Ah, family correspondence! That would have been filed in the Delay and Hold tray. I only deal with personal matters twice a year. It does lead to the occasional hiatus but at least it's ordered.' He regarded me through narrowed lids. 'Talking of personal matters, I wanted to ask you about Lady Mountjoy.'

'Mother?'

'Yes. Is she still alive?'

'Very much so.'

'That's encouraging news. Any recent sightings?'

'I had breakfast with her this morning.'

He was patently astonished. 'She's starting to *eat* again?'

'Not exactly,' I explained, 'but she's discovered a cocktail with a bacon and egg flavour. The doctor says it's a sip in the right direction.'

'Delighted to hear it. Do give her my regards, please.'

'Yes, father.'

'I'm sure she'll remember me.' A glazed look appeared. 'Yes, a fine woman, your mother. Used to see a lot of her. In fact, on three occasions I saw *all* of her.' He focused on me again. 'Incidentally, how are your brother and sister?'

'Fine. Barnaby is married now.'

'Yes. I was sorry to miss the wedding. One of the penalties of my filing system. I only got the invitation six weeks after the ceremony . . . What of Davinia?'

'She's busy finding herself, father.'

'Why? Was she lost?'

'I was speaking figuratively.'

'You are the children of a wonderful mother,' he announced with an uncharacteristic surge of sentiment. 'Lady Mountjoy is the salt of the earth. The pride of the country. She is a brick.'

I recalled their first meeting when mother had been several bricks. An entire wall, in fact. An Eton Wall. It brought me back to the matter in hand and I made a tentative start.

'I have some bad news for you, father.'

'You have to go already?'

'No . . . '

'It's been so nice to have this chat,' he said, pumping my arm. 'We must do this more often. Why don't we make it an annual event?'

'There's something I have to say to you.'

'Can't it keep for another twelve months?'

'I'm afraid not. The bad news concerns Eton.'

'Not another damn by-pass scheme!'

'I have left the College, father.'

'Well, you can't expect to stay there for the rest of your life.'

'I was expelled.'

'Good,' he rejoined with a smile. 'I was hoping you would be.'

'But I've brought disgrace on the family name.'

'Nonsense! It was Barnaby who did that.'

'Barnaby?'

'Yes. He was the only Mountjoy *not* to be expelled from Eton. What made it worse was that he went on to become Captain of the Oppidans and win several scholastic prizes. Yes, your brother has been a sore disappointment to me, Christopher. You at least have the decency to uphold the Mountjoy tradition.'

'Is that what I did, father?'

'Of course. Your expulsion was an act of justified rebellion.'

'Against what?'

'Against Eton and all that it stands for, my boy. Against that holy fool who founded the damn place.'

'Henry VI?'

'Until his lunatic reign, generations of Mountjoys held one of the most coveted and rewarding positions in the whole realm. I speak of the Mastership of the King's Whores. Henry abolished the post in a fit of religiosity and deprived us of our birthright.' A glint came into his eye. 'Just think how valuable that Mastership would be today.'

'But we don't have a king.'

'Precisely. There would be unlimited flexibility. Not to mention certain fringe benefits.' He gave me a proud grin. 'You did the right thing, Christopher. In being expelled from Eton, you were only getting your revenge on behalf of the family. I salute you.'

'Thank you, father.'

'As long as it was done honestly,' he added.

'Honestly?'

'It didn't involve murder, arson or the impersonation of a Chelsea pensioner, did it? Those crimes are strictly forbidden.'

'It was nothing like that,' I promised him.

'Good.'

'It was . . . immorality.'

'That was my chosen exit as well.'

'It had nothing to do with choice, father.'

'How disappointing!'

'I was the victim of circumstance.'

'Say no more, Christopher.'

'What happened was this, you see. Mr Dexter invited me to –'

'Enough!' he decreed. 'We are veil-drawers when it comes to lubricious detail. Do it, by all means. Watch it, draw it, film it, enjoy it in any way you please. But do not talk about it.'

'I won't, father.'

'Suffice it to say that you have done your duty at Eton.' He rubbed his hands together. 'Right! We must now sort your future out for you. What next?'

'I was rather hoping to lie fallow for a bit.'

'*Fallow*? A Mountjoy?'

'It's just under a year to my eighteenth birthday. When I

come into my inheritance – the money from Great-Aunt Lucy – I intend to travel.'

'I have other plans for you, my boy,' he asserted. 'Next term, you will go to university.'

'But I want to finish with formal education.'

'You will, Christopher. I'm sending you to Oxford. You'll be well-protected there from any formal education.'

'I could never get into Oxford!' I exclaimed.

'The traffic is a problem, I must confess.'

'Father, I'm not really an academic. I hate bookwork.'

'You sound ideally suited to the place.'

'Even though I've been expelled from a major public school?'

'I was expelled. So was your grandfather. So was every other red-blooded Mountjoy. Yet we all got into Oxford. And so will you. The only decision that has to be made is – which college?'

'But, father –'

'Barnaby went to Pembroke Dock College. Unsavoury place. He got a First. I went to Maudlin myself. No, you'd have too many hangovers in the beer cellar there. Wakefield Trinity perhaps? I suppose there's always Nearly New . . . '

'No college would take me,' I argued. 'I could never hope to pass the entrance examination.'

'That is precisely the reason that you will not be taking an entrance examination. Now leave everything to me. I simply have to make a few judicious telephone calls to see who comes up with the most attractive offer.'

'People don't get into Oxford that way!'

'People don't: Mountjoys do.'

Twenty minutes later, he had proved his point.

It was all arranged. Out of Eton and into Oxford. Out through a front door and in through a back door. Out of callow youth and into full manhood.

Out of the frying pan and into the fire.

I fell in love with Oxford as soon as I saw it. There was

such a ridiculous blend of the quaint and the contemporary. Historic buildings rubbed shoulders with vulgar, brightly-lit shops. Shuffling students shared the pavements with bustling housewives. The cloistered calm of the colleges was only yards away from the maelstrom of traffic. Books were sold alongside bacon. Intellect and industry coexisted. Heritage and progress had worked out a rough understanding.

Oxford was the sort of place where you could walk through the seventeenth century into a new car park. It was delectable.

Sir Joshua Flusher was a living embodiment of the place. He was a venerable academic in a denim suit, one of yesterday's men who owned today's Rover. Looking spruce and well-fed, this distinguished old character took me gently through my initial interview. Sir Joshua was the Master of Corpus Delicti College and it turned out that he was a close friend of father's. It has to be said that he denied the acquaintance at first but when father waved his chequebook at him, the Master recalled him at once.

While every other student had to face the rigours of an Entrance Exam, I had a leisurely stroll with a white-haired sage. As we walked towards land set aside for the new Mountjoy Annexe, he turned to me with a kind and reassuring smile.

'Now, young man. What do you intend to read?'

'I've just bought myself a new Dick Francis,' I said, trying to impress him with my eagerness. 'After that, it's a choice between Len Deighton and Jackie Collins.'

'What *subject* do you intend to read?' he clarified.

'I'm quite happy to rely on your advice, Sir Joshua. What would you recommend?'

'From what I hear, Greats might be appropriate,' he observed with the utmost discretion. 'Let us be serious. Science and Languages were not your strong points at Eton. Geography, too, I feel, is out of the question. Law would be beyond you. History would be above your head. And Sociology, quite frankly, would be beneath you.'

'What does that leave?' I asked. 'PPE?'

'FTI.'

'Financial Times Index?'

'Forestry, Theology and Industrial Archeology. A subtle mixture that is all our own. It combines fresh air with regular churchgoing and an appreciation of those less fortunate than ourselves. Oh yes, Mr Mountjoy – so kind of your father to donate that money – I am certain that FTI is for you.'

'In that case, Sir Joshua, I'll have a bash.'

'A wise decision. Apart from anything else, you have more or less guaranteed yourself a degree.'

'Why is that?'

'Because no student of FTI has ever had to take Finals. In the course of three years, you will either be injured by a falling tree, undergo a spiritual crisis or have a mental breakdown as a result of exposure to the fumes – I speak metaphorically – of heavy industry. Like every other student before you, Mr Mountjoy, you will be awarded a degree *in aegrotat*.'

'What's that, Sir Joshua?'

'In bed. It is a Latin phrase to denote illness or disability.' He permitted himself a congratulatory smile. 'I should perhaps tell you that I am a classicist. Greece and Rome are my touchstones.'

'I hope to go on a package tour to Athens one day,' I confided.

'Fifty years ago, I went on a package tour of the Ancient World,' he declared, 'and I have never returned.'

'I should complain to your travel agent.'

'My mind, Mr Mountjoy. I refer to my mind. To this day, it is still with Homer and Virgil. With Tacitus and Caesar Book Five.'

I wondered what Homer would make of the Master's new Rover or his Rolex watch or the personal stereo in his top pocket or his gold-framed spectacles. Sir Joshua read my thoughts.

'Material possessions mean nothing.'

'Don't they?'

He tapped his forehead. 'MENS SANA IN CORPORE SANO.'

'PRO BONO PUBLICO,' I replied to show him that I had some grasp of the lingo. 'VOX POPULI.'

I soon regretted my mistake. I set him off like a Roman candle.

'In life, young man, we move A POSSE AD ESSE – from the possible to the actual. Make the right decisions. LIBERIUM ARBITRIUM – free choice – is a virtue. HONOR EST IN HONORANTE – honour is in him who honours. Avoid VENALE PECUS – the venal herd. Remember that LABOR OMNIA VINCIT – work conquers all. Also, MIRABILE DICTU – strange to relate – BONA BONIS CONTINGUNT – good things befall the good. FINIS.'

I had only one shot left. The family motto.

'NON SEQUITUR.'

He was rocked. 'That's a new one on me, Mr Mountjoy. I shall have to look it up in my dictionary.' He offered me a frail hand and I shook it gently. 'Well, that's it . . . '

'The interview is *over*?'

'I think so. Don't you?'

'But there must be dozens of questions you want to ask.'

'Your father has already answered them.'

'Don't you want some proof of my academic ability?'

'I understand that the cheque is already in the post.'

He led me back through the quadrangle to the lodge and then waved me off. I remembered something and turned to call.

'By the way, Sir Joshua! When does Michaelmas Term start?'

'When would suit you?'

Corpus Delicti was going to be an obliging sort of place.

Long, empty months now stretched in front of me before I was due to go up to Oxford. I filled them with work, play, visiting friends, helping Nanny Groat in the garden and decorating my room. Though I caught an occasional glimpse of mother as she returned empty bottles to the Off Licence, I saw nothing at all of father. Having got me into Corpus Delicti, he had fallen away like a booster rocket.

Davinia, too, was conspicuous by her absence. The Fast Car Brigade continued to call for her and the butler had to issue daily bulletins as to her whereabouts. She was touring the Continent and I envied her. My urge to travel was greater than ever but the furthest that I managed to get during the whole holiday was to London.

It was not my most successful visit to the metropolis.

'Barnaby?'

'Who is this?' His telephone manner was brusque.

'Christopher. Your brother.'

'What do you want?'

'I just rang to say hello.'

'Hello,' he conceded. 'Is that all? I'm busy.'

'I'm having a week in London,' I explained. 'It seemed like an ideal time for us to meet up.'

'Why?'

'So that we can see each other.'

'We saw each other only three and a half months ago. I don't think we should overdo these things.'

'But I'm your *brother*,' I reminded him.

'You're not after money, are you?'

'Of course not.'

Horror entered his voice. 'Or somewhere to stay?'

'No. I simply wanted to . . . touch base. I come to London so rarely, it's silly not to make the effort to see you while I'm here.' There was a guarded pause at the other end of the line. 'How are your mornings looking?'

'Full.'

'Afternoons?'

'Packed.'

'That leaves the evenings.'

'We go to bed very early.' He rose to a token politeness. 'Look, why not give me a ring next time you're in town?'

'But that may not be for ages, Barnaby!'

'I can wait.'

'Don't you *want* to see me?' I asked plaintively.

'Thanks for calling!'

He put down the receiver with brotherly love.

The offhand treatment was no more than I had expected. Left to myself, I would not even have bothered to make contact with him but mother had made a particular point of asking me to do so. For her sake, therefore, I tried again.

'Is Barnaby Mountjoy there, please?'

'Are you his brother?' The voice was cold, fortyish, secretarial.

'May I speak to him?'

'He is not in the office at the moment.'

'Can you tell me when he will be?'

'No.' She had been primed to keep me at bay. 'I'm afraid I can't.'

'Will you take a message, then?'

'Only if it's urgent.'

'Could Barnaby just spare me five minutes one lunchtime?'

'No.'

'Why not?'

'Mr Mountjoy has a business lunch at the Charing Cross Hotel every day. He has no free time for the next seven months. Please do not trouble him again.'

It was the second time someone had hung up on me.

I decided on a compromise. I would lurk outside the hotel at lunchtime and exchange the briefest of greetings as he went past. That would discharge my duty and appease mother. I was staying at a flat in Garrick Street. It was one of many properties that father owned in the city and it was used on a regular basis by Davinia. Her traces were everywhere. The bathroom was a cosmetics counter and the bedroom had been turned into a kind of boudoir-cum-gallery. It was arrestingly feminine and lined with photographs of her conquests.

At twelve-thirty, I walked from the flat to the hotel and got there just in time to see Barnaby climb out of a taxi. He was in his usual black pinstripe suit and carried a briefcase. I followed him as he went into the hotel, up the stairs to the first floor and into a room. Evidently, he was having his business luncheon in private.

I arrived earlier the next day but so did Barnaby. Once again I was unable to catch him as he entered the hotel, ascended the stairs and let himself into the same room. I lurked in the corridor for almost an hour this time but no food was brought. It was difficult to believe that a self-important civil servant like my brother would carry sandwiches in his briefcase.

Curiosity took me back on the third day and the routine was the same. Taxi, hotel, stairs, first floor room. Telling myself that I must not let mother down, I confronted him when he finally came out.

'Barnaby?'

'What the devil do *you* want!'

'Mother was hoping we might bump into each other.'

'I have to get back to the office!' he snapped.

'Can I ask you one question?'

'No.'

'Why do you go into that room every lunchtime?'

He glowered at me. 'For tax purposes.'

He pushed past and went down the stairs. I was about to leave myself when I heard the door of the room open. A smart, businesslike young woman came out. No slit skirt. No heavy make-up. No earthy appeal. She was flicking through a sheaf of credit card counterfoils. My suspicions had been ignoble. Barnaby *had* been in there discussing his finances with a tax consultant.

As I left the hotel and went up the Strand, only one thing puzzled me. Why had the young woman walked on down the corridor and let herself into another room? The answer soon came. The tax consultant had a suite of offices at the hotel. After solving Barnaby's problem, she went off to straighten out another client.

Though I did my best to see all I could while I was in

London, I still felt very lonely and lacked the skill to strike up casual friendships. I was overjoyed, therefore, when Rosemary Anne rang me up at the flat. Gordy had told her that I was in London. Since she would be there herself to do some shopping on Saturday, would it be possible for us to meet up? I arranged to meet her in the afternoon. It was only after I put down the telephone that the significance of the arrangement hit me.

It would be the first time we had really been alone together.

I met her outside Liberty's, relieved her of her parcels and took her to a restaurant. Over tea and cakes we caught up on each other's news. She was anxious to have certain facts corroborrated.

'I felt sure that Gordy must have got it wrong.'

'No. That – in essence – is what happened.'

'You mean that Mrs Dexter tried to – ?'

'I'd rather not go into the gory details, Rosemary Anne.'

'It must have been dreadful!'

But even as she was expressing sympathy, I could see that she was somehow impressed with me. It was as if the incident at Eton had shifted me to sudden maturity. I basked in her approval.

'What time do you have to go home?'

'No hurry, Christopher. Why?'

'I wondered if we might grab a film . . . '

'Super idea!'

We hurried off, bought a paper and made our choice.

Five minutes after the film started, Rosemary Anne slipped her hand into mine. Ten minutes later, I lost all interest in what was up on the screen. Fifteen minutes after that, she leaned over and whispered in my ear.

'Christopher . . . '

'Yes?'

'I'm not really enjoying this.'

'Sorry,' I said, pulling my hand guiltily away.

'Not *that*, silly!' she giggled. 'The film.'

'Oh.'

'Do you like it?'

'Stopped watching ages ago.'

There was a pause. 'How far away is your flat?'

As we walked along Shaftesbury Avenue, I kept reminding myself to take the initiative. Rosemary Anne would expect it. She had begun the hand-holding and got us out of the cinema and pointed us towards the flat. The rest was up to me. Years of loving and longing could finally be resolved in the only way possible. I wanted her and I sensed that she wanted me.

'Do you remember Carlotta Nashe?' she asked.

'Vaguely.'

'She used to fancy you like mad.'

'Did she?' I was pleased at how surprised I sounded.

'I told her that she was wasting her time.'

She squeezed my hand and we both lengthened our stride. Without knowing it, Rosemary Anne was giving me the opportunity to burn Carlotta out of my memory. This would be no wild grope in a hay-loft. It would be the real thing. Hearts and flowers. And bodies.

When we reached the flat, I inserted the key in the lock with a trembling hand. Rosemary Anne kissed me lightly on the cheek.

'I was hoping you'd ask me back.'

'Were you?'

'I didn't *have* to come to London today.'

'You mean . . . ?' It was exactly as I had always dreamed it would be. 'How long can you stay?'

'There's a late train.'

Initiative was now surging inside me and I almost dragged her into the flat. In my eagerness and excitement, I did not notice the untidy state of the living room or the empty champagne bottles that were scattered about. I was there to claim a prize for which I had now been waiting for a very long time. Nothing was going to hold me back now.

I took her into the bedroom to ease her down on the bed.

'Oh my God!' she said.

The bed was occupied. Very occupied.

One young woman and two young men. All naked and all fast asleep. The air was still charged with unbridled passion. The bed looked used.

When the young woman opened her eyes, I mustered what self-control I could and turned to Rosemary Anne.

'I don't think you've met my sister, Davinia, have you?'

Chapter Seven:
UP AT OXFORD

Corpus Delicti College stands between the imposing Merkin College and the almost overpowering Christ Almighty! College. There has been much crude speculation as to how the former got its name but with the latter we are on firmer ground. Its intended nomenclature was Christ Church but the foundation stone slipped from its ropes as it was about to be laid and landed on the foot of the dignitary who was making the speech. His apt response has been enshrined for ever in the name of this vast, meandering, architectural maze.

I was glad that I was in a small college. It felt homely.

'Mr Mountjoy?'

'Yes, that's right.'

'Top bloody room, first bloody staircase!'

'Thank you.'

'Dinner at bloody eight!'

'I'll be there.'

'Bloody good grub. *Too* bloody good for you bloody students!'

The College Porter was a cheery fellow.

Dinner on the first day of Michaelmas Term was served in the refectory, an oak-panelled room that was lined with portraits of former masters. In some ways there were overtones of Eton but the place differed considerably in one particular. Its sound. Instead of the uniform twang of the Etonian accent, I heard voices from all over the provinces. Set against these distinctive regional noises was the occasional public school drawl but we were very much in the minority. I liked that. I was ready for a change.

The chatter was largely about the college itself and it soon became clear that Corpus Delicti had its idiosyncrasies.

'They have a Professor of Comparative Philately here.'

'And a Reader in Polish Demonology.'

'They've got two Lecturers in Pure and Applied Basket Weaving.'

'Then there's the Senior Tutor in Psychotic Geography . . . '

Another unique feature was Sir Joshua Flusher, our genial Master from the Ancient World. He gave us a charming speech of welcome and told us of Corpus Delicti's family atmosphere.

'Let us hope it will continue to be a happy family,' he said, raising his glass to us. 'In conclusion, gentlemen, one final point. It cannot have escaped your notice that this college is exclusively male.' Polite laughter down the tables. 'It is important to keep it that way. Ladies are very welcome during visiting hours – two o'clock until four every afternoon – but at no other time.' He lowered his head to peer over the gold-framed spectacles. 'This is not a common motel, gentlemen. If you feel you must – do it somewhere else!'

He could not have put it more plainly than that.

After recent events I was glad that I was not in a mixed college. I would now be safe from temptation and able to keep myself pure for Rosemary Anne. That, at least, was the theory.

In practice, it would not turn out quite like that.

Since FTI comprised three subjects, I had expected three separate tutors but Corpus Delicti opted for a more compact approach. They came up with the one man in Oxford who could teach Forestry, Theology and Industrial Archeology with equal assurance. Chuck Novis was a former Canadian lumberjack who lived – without scandal – in a *ménage à trois* with two unfrocked French Catholic priests and who supplemented his income by working as a nightwatchman at Cowley Motor Works.

Chuck was something of a rough diamond.

'What made you guys choose something as dumb as FTI?'

'Sir Joshua advised me,' I explained.

'And me,' mumbled Ferriday.

'Flusher is a fink,' opined our tutor. 'He doesn't know his arse from his Aristotle.'

Chuck was a huge, hulking man in check shirt and jeans. With his mocking, gap-toothed grin and his Desperate Dan shaving habits, he seemed slightly out of place in the study of an Oxford College.

'Okay!' he decided. 'Lemme tell you what you're gonna need. Forestry – get yourselves an axe and a coil of rope.'

'Yes, sir,' I replied.

'Yes, sir,' muttered Ferriday.

'The name is Chuck and it rhymes with fuck! Got it?'

'Yes, Chuck,' I said.

'Yes, Chuck,' murmured Ferriday.

'Speak up, Ferriday!' roared the Canadian.

'Yes, Chuck,' returned the other, marginally louder.

Ferriday was the only other student of FTI. He was a strange, thin, pale, introverted young man and he was clearly terrified of Chuck Novis. Even though Ferriday was a Wykehamist, I felt sorry for him. He was used to a gentler academic approach.

'Theology!' continued Chuck. 'All you need is these.'

He threw us each a copy of the Gideon Bible. When I glanced inside the cover of mine, I saw that it had come from the Holiday Inn in Toronto.

'Industrial Archeology – buy yourselves a fucking spade!' He gave us the gap-toothed grin. 'That just about wraps it up for today, guys. Any questions?' Without giving us a moment to ask any, he swept on. 'Good. First tutorial – next goddamn Monday at ten. Be there.'

He hurried us to the door and shunted us out. As we walked down to the quadrangle, Ferriday looked as if he was suffering from first degree culture shock. I tried to cheer him up.

'Chuck seems amiable enough. Tutorials should be fun.'

'Who for?' he asked lugubriously.

'I thought he took a refreshingly different approach to study.'

'Why does he have to keep chewing that gum?'

Ferriday was not the most exciting companion with whom to begin my career at Oxford but I found it difficult to shake him off. He followed me wherever I went and seemed to draw strength from me. That afternoon we went to the Freshers' Fair together. It was a boisterous event held in the Town Hall and designed to recruit new undergraduates into the university's various clubs and societies. Stalls had been set up and barkers competed noisily. I was soon caught up in the exhilaration and joined several things in the spirit of friendship.

Silent throughout, Ferriday at last confided his secret.

'I'd love to join OUDS.'

'Then go ahead, old chap.'

'Will you join as well, Mountjoy?'

'But I'm not interested in drama.'

'I'll join if *you* join,' he insisted. '*Please*!'

I did not have the heart to refuse. We paid our money and were given membership cards by a vivacious girl in a red sweatshirt. She drew our attention to the auditions for the forthcoming major production of *King Lear* and invited us to come along. We thanked her and went off into the crowd again.

We spent a few minutes listening to a wild-eyed undergraduate telling us why we should pelt the American embassy with plastic replicas of President Reagan. It was earnest, well-intentioned stuff but I found it rather lowering for a Saturday afternoon. As I was about to move away, Ferriday gripped my arm.

'I'm glad that Corpus Delicti is not a mixed college, aren't you?'

'Well . . . '

'That's why I chose it.'

'Oh.'

'Girls frighten me.'

Before I could ask him why, he spun on his heel and vanished into the throng. Ten minutes later, he reappeared again with a shy grin of apology. We headed back towards the college.

'Can I ask you a favour, Mountjoy?'

'Of course, old chap.'

'Will you hear me?'

'I can hear you, Ferriday. Loud and clear.'

'I want you to hear me do some speeches.'

'They're not about plastic replicas of President Reagan, I hope?'

'No. They're from *King Lear*. Will you?'

'If you wish.'

'I'll come to your room after dinner.'

During the meal itself, Ferriday was his usual subdued self. He contributed nothing to the animated conversation going on all around him. As dessert was being served, he got up and left the refectory without a word, returning ten minutes later with the same shy grin that I had collected from him earlier.

He joined me in my room after dinner and handed me the Arden edition of *King Lear.* Slips of paper marked key speeches by all the main characters. I braced myself. Since I had not as yet heard him raise his voice much above a nervous whisper, I could not understand how he had the courage to tackle Shakespeare. The play called for booming delivery and not for his Wykehamist mutter.

'Are you ready, Mountjoy?'

'Fire away!' I said, fearing the worst.

'I'll do Edmund first . . .'

And so he did. The next half-hour was a revelation. Ferriday knew all the speeches by heart and he declaimed them with great feeling. His shyness had gone completely and his slight frame seemed to grow and fill out. He had poise and authority and spoke the verse quite beautifully in a voice that could have reached the back of an aircraft hanger. Ferriday was a born actor. When the performance was over, I clapped enthusiastically.

'That was marvellous!'

'Thanks,' he said, his old insecure self again.

'You've done this sort of thing before.'

'Once or twice.'

'What did you play?'

'I was Henry V at Winchester.'

I was impressed. Admittedly, it *was* only Winchester but the chap did have the title part. One of the longest in Shakespeare, in fact. I wondered if he had managed to get through it without doing his now celebrated disappearing trick. An audience could get restive if their soldier-king left the stage for ten minutes in the middle of the Crispin Day speech and you would not win the Battle of Agincourt with an apologetic grin.

'I want to audition for *Lear*,' he confessed.

'You're bound to get a part, Ferriday. Two parts. Three. The whole lot. When they hear what I've just heard, they'll probably ask you to do the play as a one-man show.'

'Will you audition as well, Mountjoy?'

'Me?'

'I couldn't possibly do it without you.'

'But I don't even like the play. Not enough laughs.'

'Please, Mountjoy. It would mean so much to me.'

'I'll come along and hold your Arden for you,' I offered.

'That's not enough. You must be in the production.'

'But I don't stand a chance of getting a part. They wouldn't even cast me as part of the scenery.'

'At least say that you'll try.'

'It would be a waste of time.'

'But you'll come?'

I shrugged. 'I'll see . . . '

'Thank you, Mountjoy! Thank you!'

'All I've said is that I'll see.'

'That means yes.'

Ferriday was getting to know me.

The production of *King Lear* was to be the dramatic highlight of the term. It would run for a week at the Oxford Playhouse and it was to be directed by no less a figure than Lance Arundel. Everyone wanted to be in it. Bookshops sold out of texts of the play and there was a subsequent rush on throat lozenges. It was a long time since an Oxford University Dramatic Society production aroused such universal interest and the explanation lay in the choice of director.

Lance Arundel was a megastar.

He was that phenomenon of our times – a pop professor. A media personality who was seen on television more often than in the Senior Common Room. A trend-setting intellectual who made education seem like a high-minded episode of *Dallas*.

Ruthless, ambitious but undeniably brilliant, Lance Arundel had made his name by his remarkable fusion of the Two Cultures. For his genius in producing a workable synthesis between Art and Science, he had been awarded a Chair at the age of thirty. Now, as Professor of Literate Physics, he brought the music of the humanities to the laboratory and was the only man in academic history to give a lecture on electricity in blank verse and then follow it with a talk on Jacobean Poetry that was delivered in pitch darkness.

He was a showman and *King Lear* was his next show.

'It will run for a month.'

'A year!'

'A decade!'

'We'll transfer to the West End.'

'To Broadway.'

'To Hollywood!'

'This production will be a landmark in world theatre!'

The auditions. Everyone buzzing. Speculation rife.

Ferriday was shaking like an aspen as he waited to be called in to see the great man. Failure feelings licked at his soul.

'I can't go through with it, Mountjoy.'

'Of course you can, old chap.'

'But my voice has gone completely!'

'Get in there and knock him dead.'

'How?'

'Just show him your Edgar.'

When his name was called out, Ferriday went off like a man on his way to the scaffold. He was cowed by Arundel's reputation and deep in the rut of his own lack of self-esteem. Winchester had a lot to answer for. They had discharged him with some of the pieces missing.

A girl accosted me. Red Sweatshirt from the Freshers' Fair.

'Hello,' she said. 'So you decided to audition?'

'Only to help out a friend. I'm no actor myself. I'm just one of Nature's spear carriers.'

'But there won't *be* any spears in this production.'

'Why not?'

'Haven't you heard?'

'No.'

'Lance is thinking of setting the whole thing during the Russian Revolution. It will be long coats and rifles all round. He's talking about real snow for the blasted heath.'

'How will he manage that?'

'Lance can manage anything.'

That was the general feeling. The fact that he had never actually directed a play before did not matter at all. Success was guaranteed.

Lance Arundel was God with a PhD.

Ferriday emerged from his audition. He looked ashen.

'How did it go?' I asked.

'Disaster. I made a complete mess of it.'

'But you'd made a terrific Kent. Didn't you read for it?'

'I didn't read for anything!' he wailed. 'He just kept asking me questions about the Quantum Theory. What's *that* got to do with the play?' Ferriday was desperately hurt. 'Did you know that he's going to set the production in Ancient Egypt? Thinks it would make a tremendous climax if Lear fell from a pyramid in Act Five.'

'Bad luck, old chap!' I consoled.

But Ferriday was the exception to the rule. Others coming out of their auditions were in a state of euphoria. Five minutes with Arundel had enriched their lives and altered their whole perception of Bill Shakespeare. We crowded around to hear their reports.

'He made me read Cornwall as if I were Sir Edward Jenner. Instead of blinding Gloucester, I innoculated him.'

'I did the King of France as Louis Pasteur in a crown.'

'Edmund will wear armour made out of litmus paper so that when he's killed, it will turn red.'

'Lance may set the play in a branch of Boots the Chemist.'

The message was clear. Arundel was using the Bard to bring about a grotesque, morganatic marriage between Art and Science. He was conducting a live experiment on the Swan of Avon.

I was not looking forward to my turn. My predecessor was a pale, sensitive young man who floated past on Cloud Nine.

'What's he like?' I asked.

'Pure magic. The ultimate in improvisation.'

'Why?'

'Lance told me to pretend I was a wombat having a multiple orgasm. Such a sense of release!' He bent over to whisper to me. 'Don't tell the others but I think he's going to cast me as Cordelia.'

I let him sit down to recover and went off into the room.

Lance Arundel was sitting behind a table and playing with a computer. He was an arresting man with iron grey hair above a bulbous forehead and bright blue laser beams instead of eyes. Black leather covered him from head to foot. From a gold chain around his neck hung a medallion that showed H.G. Wells in conversation with the Invisible Man.

Something on the screen in front of him made Arundel smile. The laser beams searched me out. His voice was deep and persuasive.

'Hello, Christopher T. Mountjoy.'

'I only want to carry a rifle.'

'Rifle?'

'Or a fan if the play is set in Ancient Egypt.'

'Fan?'

'If you plump for Boots the Chemist, I'd be happy to come on with a large bottle of aspirins.'

'What *are* you on about?'

'Me, Professor Arundel. I don't want any lines.'

'Nonsense! It's not every day I get the chance to cast someone of your stature, Christopher. My computer has told me all about you. Mountjoy Manor. The Blue Bathroom. Eton, June the Fourth with Pretty Polly.' The laser beams intensified. 'You and I are brothers under the skin.'

'Are we?'

'We are both hunting the same Holy Grail. We want to unite two opposing elements. *I* want to prove that Literature has a scientific basis and *you* are striving to raise Biology to the level of an art. I must have you in this play.'

'But I can't act for toffee!'

'You have an immediate kinship with the majority of Equity members,' he said. 'Besides, I don't want you to *act* but to be yourself. Consider yourself cast.'

'I haven't *done* anything yet!'

'Your audition took place with the housemaster's wife. Besides, your face will fit perfectly into an Oriental setting.'

'Oriental?'

'Yes. I'll probably set the play in tenth century Japan. Lear is a sort of Shogun with an interest in chemical warfare.'

'Couldn't I just come on carrying a lacquered screen?'

'Goodbye, Christopher. Send the next one in, please.'

My audition was over. Catastrophe had been set in motion.

When Chuck Novis failed to turn up for three consecutive tutorials, I became alarmed. I expressed my concern to Sir Joshua over a glass of sherry in his study.

'Don't worry about it. Novis has only gone to Canada.'

'For good!' It might compromise my chances of getting a degree. 'Chuck said nothing to us, Sir Joshua.'

'That is in the nature of the beast, I'm afraid.'

'What is he doing in Canada?'

'Competing in the Quebec Log-Rolling Championships. We make it our policy to encourage any extra-mural activity among the Fellows that will add lustre to the college.'

'When is he due back?'

'Next term.'

'Next term! But he's our tutor, Sir Joshua.'

'I know that.'

'Our *three* tutors!'

'Novis has left plenty of suggestions as to how you and young Ferriday can occupy yourselves. I have a list somewhere.' Balancing his glass on the bronze bust of Cicero, he searched his desk top until he found a piece of paper. 'Here it is. FT and I are all covered.'

'What does he suggest for Forestry?'

'A nocturnal visit to Christ Almighty! Meadows with a chain-saw. It will teach you about the density of various timbers and the firewood will come in handy for the college boiler.'

'Theology?'

'An inspired idea. Peripatetic Self-Education.'

'How?'

'It seems that times for Communion Service vary considerably in the city. Novis has worked out how you can fit in six different churches on a Sunday morning. It will mean arriving late and leaving early in each case, of course, but you'll be able to compare the communion wine at six places. A sort of sacred pub crawl.'

That sounded like Chuck Novis. Theology by thirst.

'What about Industrial Archeology?'

'I'll have to find you the map for that, Mr Mountjoy.'

'Map?'

'You and young Ferriday are going on a treasure hunt.'

'Where?'

'All over the place. Novis has buried forty-seven parts of a 1938 Standard Vanguard at separate locations throughout the county. Your job is to find them and dig them up.'

'I see. No essays?'

'Why should Novis bury essays?'

I let it pass. Seeing that I was still disturbed, he poured more sherry on troubled waters and eased me on to a new topic.

'I hear that you have the part of the Fool in *King Lear.*'

'Yes, Sir Joshua, though heaven knows why he chose me. As an actor, I've got two left feet. My movement is wooden, my timing is hopeless and I can't learn lines to save my life. I'm going to make a complete fool of myself.'

'Ideal casting, obviously . . . '

I threw down my sherry. 'Goodbye, Sir Joshua. I'd better go and break the bad news to Ferriday.'

'Do it carefully. Young Ferriday has been struggling with FTI.'

'No more than me.'

'According to Novis, he is very weak on Forestry. Can't see the wood for the trees.' The Master drained his glass. 'You, on the other hand, are very strong on Theology.'

'Am I?' It was news to me. 'Did Chuck say that?'

'Yes. He is pleased with your progress. You're really getting the hang of swinging that incense-burner . . . '

It was good to have my efforts appreciated.

Rehearsals for the play were held every afternoon in a lecture room at Worcester Sauce College. As well as directing and rewriting, Lance Arundel was playing Lear as well and so I saw a great deal of him. His manic enthusiasm soon fired me and I actually began to enjoy my role. Then came the first costume fitting.

I was sent to a rambling old house in Crick Road near the Parks. As I climbed the stairs, I met another member of the cast coming down. He was a small, fey, winsome creature at a transitional stage of his life and he always attended rehearsals in an oil-stained boiler suit and a pair of ballet

shoes. Some of the others laughed at him but I liked the way that he delivered alternate lines of the Herald in high falsetto and basso profundo.

'Hello, Christopher,' he said with a hearty chuckle.

'Have they sorted out your Herald's costume?'

'No,' he lisped, 'but they measured me all over. It was divine.'

'I'd better go on up.'

The masculine voice dominated. 'I'll wait for you downstairs.'

I went on up to the top floor, knocked on the door then entered a room that was awash with costumes, wigs, hats, shoes, boots, gloves and rolls of material. Large mirrors stood everywhere.

There were three of them. Nan. Veronica. Barbie.

They were expecting me and I got a burst of giggling hilarity as soon as I walked in. Lance had clearly divulged the secrets of his computer. The costume department knew all about me. And it.

Who exactly said what I am not sure because they seemed to operate as a single unit. Three attractive young women in tight trousers, loose sweaters and a mood for some fun.

The first complete sentence got a belly laugh.

'Lance wants you to wear a pair of tights!'

There was a ryder.

'With a codpiece!'

And then another.

'Hand-fitted!'

The Fool was also supposed to wear a tabard and a cap and bells but there was no mention of those. Above the waist I had only limited appeal to the three gigglers. Their element was below.

'Would you like to try a few pairs of tights on?'

'She means one pair at the time.'

'We'll hold your trousers for you!'

While they had another communal fit of hysteria, I went over to a large box full of tights and began to sort through them. The girls soon joined me to add their professional advice.

'Choose a pair with plenty of give.'

'What about these? One green leg, one amber.'

'If we give him a red codpiece, he'll be able to stop traffic!'

'From what I hear, he can anyway!'

There is a limit to how much of this sort of thing you can take on a cold October afternoon. I reminded them that I was there on serious business and then pulled a pair of lurid yellow tights out of the box. It was then that I noticed there was nowhere to change.

'I'll take them away and try them,' I suggested.

'Try them here, Christopher. Don't be shy.'

'We're used to it.'

'We've just had the Duke of Burgundy stark naked in here for over an hour.'

'And we had to *pay* the Herald to put his clothes back on.'

The giggles were starting up again and so I decided to speed up my suffering. Kicking off my shoes, I undid my trousers and stepped out of them before reaching for the yellow tights.

'Take your socks off first!'

'And your underpants!'

'I'll try them on as I am, if you don't mind,' I said.

'We do mind – don't we girls?'

'YES!'

'Let's give him a hand.'

With a whoop of joy they leapt at me and grappled for my socks and jockey shorts. I managed to fight them off and run across the room but there was no escape. They were on me again like terriers, clinging, pulling, tickling, shrieking with laughter.

A cheer went up as one sock was removed. The second sock got an even louder shout. All three of them now concentrated on my shorts and I knew that I could not keep them at bay any longer.

Besides, I was enjoying it. Why should I fight off this personable trio when I could submit gratefully to their joint needs? I was just about to stop struggling and let them have their way with me when a foot jabbed me hard in a most tender place. I yelped in pain and understood how a rugby ball must feel when heeled from a scrum.

With a superhuman effort, I pushed them off and got to my feet. Dashing to a hamper, I flung it open and grabbed armfuls of material. When they came at me again, I hurled everything I could at them until the whole room was billowing. Joining happily in the spirit of it all, they grabbed tights and costumes themselves and pelted me back. It was a long time before the blizzard eased off. When it did, they had me cornered again and were determined not to miss their prize this time.

Two of them pounced and held an arm each while the third got a firm grip on my shorts. Just as she was about to remove them, the door opened and the Herald charged in. His voice was deep and manly.

'I heard screams up here. What's going on?' He took in the situation and resorted to his lips. 'Hands off, girls! He's mine!'

'Christopher is here for a fitting.'

'We were trying to find out the size of the problem.'

'To see if we could contain it.'

The giggles were half-hearted now. They let go. I was safe.

Torn between relief and disappointment, I dressed quickly then told the girls I would send them a full list of my measurements. They could work from those in the future.

As I turned to the door, The Herald beamed up at me.

'Aren't you glad I came to your rescue, Chrissy?'

'Yes,' I answered. 'Many, many thanks. To both of you.'

The Herald simpered with unabashed delight.

Even a Fool says a wise thing sometimes.

Chapter Eight: TAKING A BOW

'Good morning, Mr Mountjoy. Seven o'clock on a Wednesday, sir.'

'Good morning, Bernard.'

'Did we sleep well last night, sir?'

'Very well, thanks.'

'Young men with clear consciences always sleeps well,' he noted, putting my tea and newspaper on the bedside table. He opened the curtains to admit the light. 'Weather, dry; wind, cold; sky, cloudy; outlook, continuing much the same, sir.'

Bernard was my scout and his wizened old face had been coming around my door every morning for weeks. I loved to hear him chatter away with his soft Oxfordshire burr. It was the perfect way to get a new day off the runway.

'Forestry today, is it, sir?'

'No, Bernard. Theology.'

'Very useful subject for young men to study, sir. Makes you God-fearing, keeps you on the straight and narrow.'

'Think there's a danger of my going astray, do you?' I teased.

'Well, sir, I can't pretend I hold with this play-acting of yours.'

'*King Lear* is a famous tragedy.'

'That's as maybe, sir. But as for young men dressing up in funny clothes and cavorting about a stage . . . Well, I'm not sure it's altogether healthy, sir.'

'Why not find out? Come and see the show.'

'Heaven forbid, Mr Mountjoy! What will you suggest next?'

Oxford owes an enormous debt to its Bernards. The University could survive without its books, its buildings, its lectures, its dons and even – at a pinch – its undergraduates. But it could never pull through without its college scouts. They *are* Oxford.

'Shall I draw your bath now, sir?'

'Yes, please.'

'With or without bath salts, sir?'

'Without.' I heard him turn on the taps in the bathroom and I waited for him to reappear. 'Have you ever thought of working in a mixed college, Bernard?'

He stiffened with horror. 'I could never lower my standards that far, Mr Mountjoy. Young men and young female persons should not be put together, in my view. Leads to complications.'

'It must also add a bit of variety to the job,' I argued.

'I knows all about "variety", thank you, sir!'

'What do you mean?'

'My friend is a scout at St Catts and Doggs, sir. They're mixed. He never knows what he's going to find next when he goes into a bedroom of a morning. That's "variety" for you, sir. Last week, he goes to wake one young man and he finds five female persons on the bed. My friend nearly had a stroke.'

'Of what?' I corrected myself at once. 'Poor man!'

'Five of them! Unclothed. It wouldn't do for me, sir.'

'How many would you want, Bernard?'

'I'm serious, Mr Mountjoy. Someone has to draw the line.'

'Of course.'

'That's why I chooses my young men with care. If I thought any of them would let me down in a bedroom, sir, I wouldn't be fetching their tea and drawing their baths.'

'I take the point.'

'There aren't many of us left, sir. Those of us that are still here, have got to make a stand for decency.' He drew himself up to his full, unimpressive height. 'Will that be all, sir?'

'Yes, thank you.'

'Goodbye, sir,' he said, turning to go.

'Goodbye, Bernard. Oh, and do let me know if you change your mind about the play. I'll get you a complimentary ticket.'

By way of an answer, he shut the door firmly behind him.

Originality was the keynote of Lance Arundel's approach to *King Lear*. The play, he told us, was a parable on the murder of Art by Science. Without realizing it, Shakespeare had created in Lear the archetype of the Mad Scientist and fashioned his youngest daughter, Cordelia, into the Muse of Poetry. Goneril and Regan were really no more than senior laboratory technicians who got above themselves. Edmund, the bastard, stood for genetic peculiarity and Edgar – during his Poor Tom phase, at least – was an embodiment of British Drama, stripped bare by the cruel withdrawal of Arts Council subsidies.

It all sounded wonderfully plausible the way that he explained it. Early on in rehearsals, I asked him about my own role.

'Where does the Fool come in?'

'Upstage centre.'

'I mean, where does he fit into the scheme of things?'

'He stands between Art and Science and is crushed between the two. Instead of escaping, he unwittingly invites his own death.'

'That's rather foolish of him,' I observed.

'You follow my reasoning perfectly.'

'So the Fool is – a fool!'

'Exactly!'

Arundel had an answer to everything. I did as he instructed me, swam with the tide and enjoyed rehearsals more and more. It was a very happy company, unified by its total faith in its director and convinced that we were all heading for the greatest triumph in the history of dramatic production. Arundel did nothing by halves.

There was another reason why I loved rehearsals. Her

name was Stella Grandison and she was playing Cordelia. Stella was a first-year English student from Snilda's College. She was a beautiful English rose with the face of a Madonna and the body of a seductress. Even in her old slacks and floppy sweater, she could have tempted a saint. I drooled over her and if Bernard had been aware of my fantasies about the lovely Stella, he would have had me exorcised.

One afternoon, as I left the rehearsal room, Stella came running after me. She was like an angel on the hoof.

'Christopher, could I have a word with you?'

'Of course!'

'It's rather private,' she said coyly.

'Shall we go and have a cup of tea somewhere?'

'Not in public. Could we . . . go to your room, please?'

'Yes!' I replied. It was the emotional equivalent of winning the football pools. 'We'll only have about half an hour, I'm afraid. Visiting hours are rather strictly enforced.'

'We can do it in half an hour,' she said.

I floated on air all the way back to Corpus Delicti. As soon as we reached my room, I plugged in the kettle to make some tea and to give Stella some time to settle. She was tense and nervous and she clearly had something of real importance to tell me. Eventually, she got round to it. Asking me to sit on the sofa beside her, she took me gently by the hand and made her confession.

'Christopher . . . '

'Yes, Stella?'

'I think I'm in love.'

'That's wonderful!' I exclaimed. 'I adore you as well!'

'It's never happened to me before.'

'The first time is always rather special.'

'I simply had to speak to you about it.'

'I'm glad you did, Stella.'

'You don't mind, do you?'

'Mind! I'm delighted!'

'I knew that you'd understand, Christopher,' she said, squeezing my hand in gratitude. 'I've watched you in rehearsals. You have such a kind and sympathetic face. I felt that *you* were the person.'

'Thank you! I've watched you, too,' I admitted, taking a deep breath in preparation for our first kiss.

'Do you think I should tell him?'

'Him?'

'Lance.'

'Can't we just keep it as our little secret?'

'But I love him *so* much, Christopher!'

My jubilation was stillborn. Instead of being the object of her passion, I merely occupied Good Friend status. The convenient shoulder. I hastily rearranged my features to show less excitement and more sagacity. She wanted cool, calm wisdom from me.

'Be honest with me,' she pleaded. 'Speak your mind.'

'Lance is a trifle older than you,' I pointed out, tactfully.

'That doesn't matter at all.'

'And he is married.'

'Not any more. His second wife left him last term, apparently. Whenever she wanted to ask him for his dirty washing, he was down at the Television Centre or flying to give a lecture in America or opening a boutique.' She sighed the sigh of the infatuated. 'Lance leads such a full and vital life.'

'In that case, he won't be able to fit you in.'

'But he can, Christopher. After the first performance.'

'What?'

'He's invited me to supper at the Randolph Hotel. Lance said he wanted to make it a first night to remember.' Her smile suggested that the subtext of his remark had gone fathoms over her head. 'Do you think I should go?'

'I'm not so sure.'

'But if I did, I'd have a chance to declare my love. It would be the ideal place to do it.'

'I think Lance would agree with you there!'

'Help me, Christopher. I need advice.'

'Don't rush into a decision, Stella.'

'But he keeps pressing me for an answer.'

'Tell him you need to sleep on it.'

'For how long?'

'I'll let you know when I've worked it out!'

'Thank you!' she said and kissed me on the lips.

Bernard would have been proud of me. Instead of taking advantage of the moment, I poured her some tea and told her how much I liked her Cordelia. What I did not tell her was how much I now hated a certain person's Lear. Lance Arundel was no longer the resident Stanislavsky for me. He was simply a lecher stalking his next victim.

I determined to save her.

We dug for the best part of an hour before we struck wood. Ferriday held the lantern while I brushed away the earth with my bare hands. An owl hooted above us. We used the edge of the spade to prise open the coffin and there it was. The decaying corpse of an exhaust pipe from a 1938 Standard Vanguard. We crossed another one off our list.

Ferriday was at his most melancholy.

'I can't go on like this, Mountjoy,' he moaned. 'I just don't accept the academic validity of Chuck's teaching methods.'

'I thought this was rather clever of him.'

'Burying a rusty car part in a churchyard?'

'It combines Industrial Archeology *and* Theology.'

'We are undergraduates: not Burke and Hare!'

'Fair point.'

'Excuse me.'

He disappeared into the darkness. In the ten minutes that he was gone, I worried about him. Ferriday was unhappy at Oxford. His work gave him no satisfaction and his part in the play irked him. Arundel had cast him in the tiny part of Curan and reduced his dialogue to a single line. Ferriday felt under-appreciated.

When he came back with his shy grin, I tried to offer succour.

'What's the trouble, old chap?'

'Second thoughts.'

'About Curan?'

'I'm not so sure that he *is* the harbinger of the two cultures and the microcosm of society in decay.'

'Lance should know.'

'Shakespeare should know better.'

'There is that,' I conceded. 'On the other hand, you do play the part so well. I love the way you declaim your speech.'

'All one line of it! No, we've been gulled, Mountjoy.'

'By whom?'

'That whizzkid in black leather. He's cut everyone's part.'

'Except his own.'

'Quite. He's written in extra speeches for himself. That's my point. This is not *King Lear*. It's simply the Lance Arundel Show in iambic pentameters.'

It *was* unfair. Ferriday, the true actor, was consigned to a minor role in a production he loathed while I, with no talent to speak of, had an important part in a project that I was enjoying. I sought for a way to rally his spirits.

'What are you doing next Tuesday, Ferriday?'

'Drowning myself, probably.'

'Why not come to Twickenham with me?' I said, putting a consoling hand on his wrist. 'Just the two of us.'

'Gosh, Mountjoy!' He flushed with pleasure. 'Thanks!'

'I hoped that might buck you up.'

'It does.' A sly smile appeared. 'I thought you'd never ask.'

'Been meaning to for some time, old chap.'

'I insist on paying a half-share.'

'As you wish . . . '

'Have you decided where we'll go?'

'The North Stand.'

'Appropriate name for our hotel,' he smirked.

'We'll be right up at the back . . . ' I blenched as I heard what he had said. We were talking about very different sports. 'Look here, Ferriday. I'm on about *Twickenham*.'

'I don't mind where you choose as long as we're together.'

'The Varsity Match!'

'What's that?'

'Rugby. A game. One ball. Two teams of fifteen.'

His face fell. 'You mean . . . ?'

'Yes, I'm afraid that I do.'

'And you won't . . . ?'

'No,' I informed him. 'I'm afraid I won't.'

He looked utterly betrayed. I had enticed him to show his hand and then rejected it. Ferriday vanished for another ten minutes and never came back.

His Curan deteriorated from that moment on.

The great day began in the usual way. Bernard breezed in with my tea and my newspaper, drew the curtains, gave me his weather report and ran my bath. What was not usual was the fact that I slept through it all. In the end, my scout had to prod me awake.

'Good morning, Mr Mountjoy!'

'Morning?' I yawned. 'Already?'

'Did we get to bed late last night?' he asked, knowingly.

'Nearly three o'clock, Bernard.'

'And we both know why, don't we, sir?'

'The final dress rehearsal went on a bit, that's all.'

'I did warn you, sir. That play is undermining your health.'

'We had set problems. The screen wouldn't fit.'

'Screen, sir?'

'The production has a scientific slant, Bernard. To give the audience the feeling that they're watching an animal experiment, we've got this perspex screen across the whole proscenium arch.'

'Animal experiment? I don't like the sound of that, sir.'

'It would take too long to explain,' I said, wearily. 'The point is that the set held us up for hours. We didn't start the run until ten o'clock. Then we had costume problems.'

'Take up darts, Mr Mountjoy. Much more hygienic pastime.'

'But I like drama,' I said with another yawn. 'It's fun.'

'Call me old-fashioned if you will, sir, but I still think that play-acting is not a decent thing for a young man to do.'

'This is Shakespeare!'

'Yes, and *he's* been too well-spoken of, I reckon.'

'Aren't you going to wish me luck for the first night?'

'I'd shudder at the thought of what I might be encouraging, sir.'

He stuck to his principles and went out.

A bath revived me, breakfast restored me and a brisk stroll through the meadows put the finishing touches to my recovery. I walked over Maudlin Bridge and around to Snilda's College to meet Stella Grandison.

She came out of the Lodge in tight black pants and a floppy sweater. Animation lit up her whole face and gave her skin the texture of fine satin. I had never seen her so excited and so lovely. Stella was an English rose in full bloom.

'Did you see Lance on breakfast television this morning?'

'No,' I said.

'He was magnificent! So lucid! And penetrating! When they asked him about his own performance as Lear, he said that he was only part of a team.' Her smile broadened. 'Then he mentioned me. And you.'

'I hope Lance isn't overdoing it,' I remarked. 'He's on the Jimmy Young Show next before a dash to Birmingham for Pebble Mill at One. Don't you think he should rest before this evening?'

'Lance never rests!' she asserted with pride.

We fell in beside each other and moved back towards the bridge. The purpose of our meeting was to finalize her decision. Stella was relying on me to make up her mind for her. I told her the truth.

'Don't go to supper with Lance tonight.'

'Why not?' she asked in a hurt tone.

'Because I think he may have more than supper in mind!'

'He'll want to discuss the play in detail, naturally.'

'Lance will ask you to stay to breakfast, Stella.'

'I don't mind sitting up all night and waiting for the early reviews,' she asserted. 'As long as we're together.'

'Oh, he'll make certain that you're together!' I muttered.

She was like a lamb going innocently to slaughter and she was not making it easy for me to act as the Good Shepherd. I allowed a pause as we turned the corner then tried another approach.

'What happened last night when we got to Act Five?'

'Lance repeated one scene a few times.'

'Yes, the scene where Lear carried on the dead body of Cordelia. And it wasn't a few times, Stella. It was fourteen.'

'Lance is a perfectionist.'

'Don't you mind the way that Lear dies and falls across you?'

'He's my father!'

'Fathers lie *beside* their daughters not *on* them.'

'What are you getting at, Christopher?'

'Your safety,' I said kindly. 'It's not wise for you to go with him tonight.'

'Why not?'

'Because he'll make you give a repeat performance.'

'I wouldn't mind going through my speeches again, if that's what Lance wants. He's said how much he admires my Cordelia.'

'Especially when she's dead in his arms. That's the bit you'll have to do again, Stella. On a bed. Only Lear won't die this time. He'll come alive.'

'That's the most disgusting thing I've ever heard!' she shouted.

'*I* think it's pretty rotten of him,' I agreed.

'Not Lance: *you*! Your mind is an open sewer!'

'I was only trying to help, Stella.'

'Well, I don't need help like that, thank you!' she yelled. 'Lance would never dream of doing such a thing! You're evil, Christopher! I never want to speak to you again!'

'Does that mean I can't hold your hand during the curtain call?'

'I hate you!'

She broke into a trot and left me standing. Instead of rescuing Cordelia from her father, I had just oiled the wheels of incest. I wanted to kick myself and so I did. Hard.

Lance Arundel had been burning the candle at both ends for several months. On the first night of the OUDS production of *King Lear*, the flames met in the middle. He looked dreadful. An hour before curtain up, he sat in his dressing room and swallowed handfuls of pep pills, washing them down with neat vodka.

'Wonderful make-up, Lance!' I noted.

'What?' he murmured.

'Your face looks a hundred and five years old. Very Leary.'

'I haven't put any make-up on yet.'

I felt such a Fool.

Others flooded into the dressing room for approval, reassurance, company, therapy or the chance to worship our megastar. I went off to get into my own costume. Deprived of the fun of taking my measurements personally, the trio at Crick Road had wreaked their revenge on me. The cap and bells did not fit, the tabard was too short, the tights were too small and the codpiece – red spots on a shocking pink base – threatened to stop my circulation.

The house was full. Critics from every national newspaper were in the front row. Expectations were high. The whole enterprise was surrounded by favourable omens. Until the performance started.

Act One. Scene One. The curtain rose on the island of Dr Moreau as seen through a murky perspex screen. Gloucester, Kent, and Edmund were so far upstage as to be almost invisible. Since their dialogue had been cut, they mugged away violently. A fanfare. Enter King Lear in white jacket and trousers, brandishing a long syringe. Arundel had increased his age to about three hundred by sticking on a pair of snowy eyebrows and a long, flowing beard. Instead of representing Lear as a Mad Scientist, he looked like Santa Claus doing a part-time job as a dentist.

For the first ten minutes, the audience sat in stunned silence. They simply could not work out what was going on. The sniggers began when Arundel took his first prompt. Laughs broke out when one of his eyebrows thawed and dripped to the ground. Spontaneous applause came when part of his beard got snagged up on the bare tree.

Then I came on. The audience immediately knew where they were. After being bombarded with symbols and motifs and over-intellectualized concepts, they were back to basics. A Fool. Cue for fun.

They liked the cap and bells. They were fond of the tabard. They loved the tights. But it was the codpiece that won their hearts. Under the lights, it became a throbbing monster with German measles. They could not take their eyes off it. Harmless lines about coxcombs set them off into the proverbial gales.

It got worse from that point on. Far from witnessing one of the profoundest tragedies ever written, they were seeing a French farce with scientific trappings. Mockery undermined our confidence. Mistakes multiplied, panic set in and the prompter had a longer role than Lear himself. Arundel had elected to do the play without an interval so that – in his own words – the audience would not be let off the hook. In the event, it was we who felt the piercing metal.

Our megastar was shattered. After a lifetime of universal praise, he was quite unfitted to cope with the ridicule and derision that was reverberating around the theatre. As he stumbled offstage after another dose of it, he hissed a desperate command to his cast.

'Speed things up!'

'Even the blinding of Gloucester?'

'Just take out one eye.'

'What about the hovel scene, Lance?'

'Cut it!'

Arundel set us a good example. When he went back onstage, he increased his run rate and batted through his speeches ferociously. He achieved four sixes, eight fours and hit Act Three over the pavilion during the storm scene. But the sustained laughter was getting to him. He began to eat portions of his beard and stamp his feet like a Rumpelstiltskin with royal prerogative.

I began to fear for Stella Grandison. Every time he lurched into the wings, she would be there to offer support and encouragement.

'Ignore them, Lance! They don't know genius when they see it.'

'Supper after the show!' he gasped. 'I must have you.'

'I'll be there.'

'Wear that dress!' he insisted, looking down at Cordelia's tight-fitting white silk costume. 'To start with, anyway.'

'I'll wear whatever you ask, Lance!'

'King Lear,' called the stage manager. 'You're back on.'

Arundel went reeling onstage like a drunk and got the biggest jeer yet as he bumped accidentally into the perspex screen. The rest of the cast were crammed into the wings feeling sorry for him but my sympathy was reserved for Stella. Supper at the Randolph would be an ordeal for her. Instead of being a celebratory union in the wake of a theatrical triumph, it would be a crude assault by a Mad Scientist on an unsuspecting girl.

'Don't go with him, Stella!' I pleaded.

'Leave me alone.'

'He's only after one thing.'

'I'm not talking to you.'

'Look at the state he's in! Frothing at the mouth. Do you want to be locked in a hotel room with *that*?'

A howl of fear drew our attention back to the stage. Arundel had lost his nerve. Totally humiliated by the audience response, he took to his heels and ran off to his dressing room to bang his head against the wall. Stella rushed after him to provide comfort.

Act Four bowled along at breakneck speed then Lear was due on again. Somehow, Arundel made his entrance for the mad scene. He was superb. The auditorium was stilled as the king moved about with his mind crumbling. Arundel was not acting. He had cracked under the accumulated pressures of a disastrous night.

Even Stella became afraid of him. When she played the short scene with him in the French camp, she kept yards clear of him. Arundel had one final entrance to make. Carrying the dead body of Cordelia.

The stage manager raised the alarm.

'Lance has gone! Walked out of the stage door in full costume.'

'What do we do?' asked someone.

'Lower the curtain,' decided the stage manager.

'No,' insisted Stella, the committed trouper. 'The show must go on.'

'Who's going to carry you on?' asked the stage manager.

'Christopher!' ordered Stella. 'Do something.'

And so I did. Sweeping her up into my arms, I carried her onstage right on cue. It brought the house down. Since everyone had been expecting the king, I offered an extempore line of explanation.

'The king, I fear, hath gone and done a bunk . . .'

Terminal panic gripped the rest of the actors onstage. They forgot their lines, dropped their swords, bumped into each other, then fled into the wings pursued by baying laughter.

Worse was to come. In my arms was the loveliest creature ever to wear a see-through nylon shift over her naked body. Though nominally dead, this Cordelia was so frightened by the audience reaction that her breasts were heaving like the North Sea. Red, rounded nipples peered up at me. Thighs trembled. Toes wiggled.

Stella Grandison was so warm and wonderful to the touch that armed rebellion was set off down in the codpiece. As I lowered her gently to the ground and then stood over her, there was a sudden explosion. My codpiece shot off, my tights burst asunder, and Great Aunt Lucy came out for a piece of the action.

'It's Spotted Dick!' shouted a comedian in the audience.

Hysteria reigned and people fought for rolling-space in

the aisles. To try to save my face, someone switched the stage lights off and we were plunged into pitch darkness.

'Get off!' hissed the stage manager.

'That's not a bad idea,' I agreed.

But I had lost my bearings in the darkness. Instead of sprinting into the wings, I ran straight into the perspex screen and shattered it on impact. The lights came up to show me standing there amid a snowstorm of perspex.

Great Aunt Lucy took three bows before I got off.

Chapter Nine: HANDS OFF

It was a remarkable Christmas because I managed to have a protracted conversation with my mother. Our meeting was accidental, of course, but that is in the nature of things at Mountjoy Manor. I came upon her in the Long Corridor as she was exercising her dog on a leash.

'Hello, Christopher!'

'Happy Christmas, mother!'

'So nice of you to drop in!'

'I've been at home for three weeks, mother.'

'How lovely, dear! When do you go back?' The dog yapped at her feet. 'Oh, do be quiet, Hannibal!'

'I didn't know you had a dog, mother.'

'It was a Christmas present from your father.'

'Did you ask for it?'

'Of course. I left instructions with one of his secretaries. I said that I wanted a very small dog with all the attributes of a St Bernard – obedience, loyalty and brandy.'

'Is that why you have a poodle?'

'Hannibal is no ordinary dog, Christopher. He has been trained to balance on a small barrel of brandy and roll it towards me . . . Still! Enough of me! How is Eton?'

'I left Eton last June, mother.'

'Before the term ended?' Concern whitewashed her face. 'You were not sent home because of illness, were you?'

'No, mother.'

'And I trust you did not abscond?'

'No, mother.'

'Then why did you leave?'

'I hate to shock you but . . . I was expelled.'

'Thank goodness for that! I thought it was something serious.'

The poodle lifted its leg to relieve itself against a tombstone.

Looking as gracious and imposing as ever, mother carried an exquisite ivory fan which she opened and used from time to time. It was not an ideal accessory for such a bitterly cold part of the house but when you have come by a collection of six hundred Oriental fans, you are under some moral pressure to use them.

A pleasing aroma drifted into my nostrils. Conscious that she often had the odour of spirits on her lips, mother had commissioned a new perfume that smelled of Robinson's Barley Water. It made her inebriation seem altogether more ladylike.

'Have you seen any other members of the family?' I asked.

'Frequently. Over the years.'

'Have you seen them over Christmas, I meant?'

'No, dear. Your father is abroad.'

'Where?'

'Who knows? He is a restless spirit.' A professional aside slipped out. 'Like Courvoisier.'

'What of the others?'

'Barnaby rang me up yesterday and Davinia sent me a Christmas card. Or was it the other way around?'

'How are they?'

'Developing, Christopher. Forming their own personalities in the workaday world.'

'Is Barnaby still in the Civil Service?'

'He has just had another promotion. Something to do with taking money from people under false pretences.'

'Income tax?'

'Yes, that was it.' She nudged the dog with her toe as it attempted a repeat performance on another tombstone. 'Now, now, Hannibal. No disrespect to Archbishop Mountjoy.'

'How is Davinia? I haven't seen her since the summer.'

'She has grown very lazy, I fear.'

'Has she?'

'On her own admission, she spends a lot of time in bed.'

'That was my impression, too.'

'Of course, one has to feel sorry for the poor girl.'

'Why?'

'Because her engagement fell through.'

'I didn't know that Davinia had been engaged.'

'Very briefly. He was a famous mountaineer. They met in Switzerland when he was climbing whatever it is that famous mountaineers climb. Unfortunately, he was caught in a terrible blizzard. Two days of exposure to sub-zero temperatures. The doctor said that he would always suffer from terrible frostbite and that put an end to the engagement.'

'Did it?'

'Naturally, dear. As soon as they had an intimate moment, Davinia broke it off.' We strolled along the corridor for a while until mother thought of something. 'If you have left Eton, where are you now?'

'Oxford.'

'How amusing! Your father went to Oxford.'

'I know. Maudlin College.'

'Yes, he took me there once. Fine old place. Very characterful. Beautiful tower.' A sweet smile animated her face. 'Excellent beer cellar. I was so impressed with their bar stock that I got your father to make a donation. They were terribly grateful. Indeed, I believe it was because of that that they named a dartboard after me.'

She tossed her head as she laughed and her curly wig moved in such a lifelife way that the dog gave it a roguish wink. We carried on down the Long Corridor and she yanked the animal after her.

'What are you reading, Christopher?'

'FTI.'

'French, Turkish and Indonesian?'

'No, mother. Forestry, Theology and Industrial Archeology.'

She took it on the chin. 'I do so like these modern combinations. And that choice of subjects qualifies you for so many careers.'

Yes, I thought. Wood-cutting. Swinging an incense-burner. And digging holes all over Oxfordshire. I was starting to get a little disillusioned with FTI but I did not confide my worries to mother. It was against Mountjoy rules. In her company, one simply did not rock the boat.

'Why is this corridor so long?' she asked.

'Because it's the Long Corridor, mother.'

'That sounds logical.' She hauled on her leash as Hannibal tried to water a potted plant he was just passing. 'Mountjoy Manor is so full of unexpected features. Only yesterday, I stumbled upon a saloon bar that I had completely forgotten was there. Oh, and talking of unexpected features, have you seen Nanny Groat?'

'Yes, mother. She's in fine fettle. We had tea together.'

'In the Nursery?'

'No, in the woodshed. I left her lying in her hammock.'

'Ah, yes,' she remembered. 'Nanny is one of our gardening staff now. I watched her at work only last summer. I do so like the way she throws that anchor over the side when she parks her wheelbarrow.'

We had reached the door to her private apartments. Mother stopped, fanned herself vigorously for a moment and then beamed at me as if seeing me there for the first time.

'Have you been studying hard at Oxford?' she enquired.

'Yes, mother,' I said, feeling the blisters on the palms of my hands. 'I have had to do a lot of spadework.'

'I hope you have found some time for recreation, Christopher. It is so important, I feel. Barnaby played golf when he was at Oxford. Your father was a squash man – until I introduced him to beer. What has your main interest been?'

'Drama. I took part in a production of *King Lear*.'

'Good. I hope you showed them what a Mountjoy is made of.'

'Yes, mother.'

'This family belongs centre-stage.'

'I think I upheld that tradition,' I sighed.

'Well done! I would love to visit you at Oxford this term but I have rather a lot on. Apart from anything else, I have to spend a week being shown around the Guinness Brewery in Dublin.'

'A whole week in one brewery?'

'I believe it may be a record,' she remarked. 'However, since I can't visit you, I will make sure that Davinia does.'

'Oh no! Please? Don't bother!' I protested.

'But you *want* to see your sister, don't you?'

'Yes, of course,' I lied. 'But I wouldn't like to put her to any trouble.'

'No trouble. I'll write to her. My children should keep in touch with each other. It leads to family solidarity.'

'Yes, mother.' The coming term had just lost most of its appeal for me. 'If Davinia can't manage it, I shall understand.'

'She'll manage it. I'll see to that . . . Goodbye, dear.'

'Goodbye, mother.'

She opened the door to leave and then paused. 'Oh . . . '

'Yes?'

'That Off Licence down by the gatehouse . . . '

'You had it built for convenience, mother.'

'Do you suppose they sell dog food?'

Hannibal began to whine piteously. She dragged him purposefully into the room and closed the door behind her.

Hilary Term began with a sizeable fall of snow that was deep and crisp and even until the students returned. Corpus Delicti looked like something off a Christmas card and gave promise of a yuletide retrospective. The snow caused severe problems for Ferriday and me. While other students pursued their chosen disciplines in the warmth of libraries, we were out felling timber, comparing Communion wines and digging for buried treasure. It took the shine off our studies. I wondered if Sir Joshua would let me change to Emetic Psychology.

Oxford now took a very different view of Christopher Mountjoy. After my performance in *King Lear*, I was a celebrity. Town and gown alike rippled with pleasure whenever I came along and my pigeon-hole was crammed with letters every day.

Offers from Interested Females were legion.

'Good morning, Mr Mountjoy.'

'Good morning, Bernard.'

'I've brought your mail up,' he said, dropping envelopes all over the floor. 'And I've also brought my box of matches.'

'Some of the letters are usually quite diverting, Bernard.'

'Filth. Unwanted correspondence is always filth.'

'What about all those from the Readers' Digest?'

'Burn them, Mr Mountjoy,' he urged, kicking the letters about on the carpet. 'Commit them to the flame.'

'But I haven't read any of them yet.'

'You've read more than enough already, sir. My young gentlemen should have no truck with perverts.'

'They're not *all* perverts,' I told him. 'Some of them want to do it in the conventional way.'

'Shameless hussies!'

Bernard was a small man with a big heart. Ostensibly there to look after my room and my needs, he had taken on responsibility for my soul. He liked to think that he alone stood between me and a life of corruption and depravity. And, of course, he was right.

I reached down to gather up some of the envelopes and began to open them. Bernard watched me with a box of matches in his hand.

'No more dirty photos, is it, sir?'

'Not so far.'

'No more items of female clothing?'

'Not so much as a Marks and Spencer's bra.'

'What about other "enclosures", sir?' he asked, making the word sound rich with sinister possibilities.

'Not a sniff.'

'What I can't understand, Mr Mountjoy, is why you're getting all this filth through the post every day.'

'Because my codpiece broke in Act Five.'

'No, sir,' he insisted. 'That was not you. It was someone trying to impersonate you. To blacken your good name.'

'I keep telling you, Bernard. It was *me* playing the Fool.'

'It was your double, sir. A young gentleman of mine just wouldn't *do* such a thing. Now, if it had been Mr Ferriday . . .' he said, knowingly.

'Ferriday?'

'I could believe it of him, sir. *He* might have done it.'

'But Ferriday only had one line.'

'Lines didn't come into it, sir. From what I hear, your double was not so much an actor as a stand-up comedian.'

'It wasn't Ferriday, I can tell you that. He was playing Curan. His part just wasn't big enough.'

'I still has my suspicions about that young man, sir.'

'He could never have carried Cordelia on stage,' I argued. 'Miss Grandison was a big girl. Lot of her, you see. Ferriday's too puny.'

'His room-mates are not, sir.'

'What?'

'I say no more, sir, except that I'm glad *I* don't look after him. Mr Ferriday wouldn't pass muster with me. Too unwholesome.' He threw open my bedroom window to admit an icy blast. 'Fresh air, sir?'

When I stopped shivering, I opened another envelope.

'Anything else, Mr Mountjoy?'

'No thanks, Bernard.'

'I'll leave you to it, then, sir.'

'Yes. Goodbye . . .' He headed for the door. 'WAIT!'

'You've gone all white, sir.'

'Take this!' I yelled, offering him the card I had just read. 'Burn it. Scatter the ashes in a rubbish tip.'

'More unclean suggestions, is it?'

'Yes!'

'More foul invitations from a female person?'

'Yes, yes!'

'Does she want to come here and do her dirtiest?'

'Yes, yes, yes!'

He snatched the card from me. 'Who sent it, Mr Mountjoy?'

'My sister, Davinia.'

Bernard's eyebrows hit a new altitude record. 'Incest!' he gasped.

Taking out his box of matches again, he shook it violently as if it were a charm to ward off evil spirits then he left the room and thundered down the stairs. If he had dared to read the card before he burned it, he would have seen that Davinia had written to say that she would be visiting me in Oxford.

It was the foulest missive yet from my mailbag.

The fiasco which had ruined Lance Arundel's reputation had made mine. In a small college like Corpus Delicti, I now bulked large. The Master was not certain whether to condemn or congratulate and so he did neither but sat instead on the fence with a bottle of Bristol Cream and a brochure from Swans Hellenic Cruises. The dons were with me to a man and Chuck Novis told me that I was the best thing to happen to the college since one of its Fellows secured the much sought-after Chair of Acupuncture after a needle-match with someone from Merkin.

To the other undergraduates, I became a cult figure with practical value. It became normal procedure for them to visit me when their girlfriends called. After five minutes in my company, it seemed, a couple could get up sufficient head of steam to keep themselves amused for hours. Had Bernard realized that I was acting as a kind of sexual trampolene on which assorted couples could bounce, he would have reduced my room – with me in it – to flames.

For the sake of collegiate spirit, I did not mind providing the service at first but it soon became irksome. When there was yet another knock on my door one afternoon, I resolved that it would be the last.

'Come in!' I called.

When the couple entered, I sat up in horror.

'Hello, Christopher!' greeted Neil Blythe. 'Let me introduce you to Emmeline Partridge.'

'Delighted to meet you!' she said as if in the presence of royalty. 'I've been on at Neil for ages to get us both together.'

'Could we just have five minutes of your time, old chap?'

Still speechless, I waved them to the sofa.

Neil Blythe was our rowing Blue, a huge, musclebound individual with a boyish enthusiasm and a jingoistic love for his country and its values. Had he been a stick of rock, it would have said 'England' all the way through. I had always found him amiable and harmless. Until now. Clearly, there was a darker side to his personality.

Emmeline Partridge was tiny. Neatly dressed in dark blue slacks and sweatshirt, she had a sweet little face that was set off by an explosion of blonde curls. Her glistening blue eyes were fixed on me.

'Nice day for it,' observed Neil.

'It's very cold out,' I muttered.

'We like a nip in the air,' said Emmeline. 'Makes us work that bit harder to get up a sweat.'

I was frankly scandalized. The thought of this giant young man in bed with this miniature young woman was appalling. One wrong or impulsive move and Neil could suffocate her. If not worse. I refused to be party to any of it. Sounding like Bernard, I put my foot down very firmly.

'Don't do it!' I warned.

'But we must, old chap,' he said.

'We do it every afternoon,' she added.

'It's dangerous!' I shouted.

'That's part of the fun of it, Christopher,' he said. 'Actually, I've been lucky with injuries myself. All I've done is to pull a hamstring.'

'Neil does rather throw himself into it,' said Emmeline, looking at him with admiration. 'The wonder is that he hasn't done himself more serious damage.'

'But what about *you*?' I asked her.

'I did pull a muscle in my shoulder once.'

'Doesn't it *hurt*?'

'Not any more.'

'I don't mean your shoulder,' I explained. 'When you and Neil . . . do it, aren't there any unpleasant consequences?'

'An occasional sore throat, that's all.'

I tried to censor the picture that flashed into my mind but it remained there to torment me. Evidently, Neil was not just taking advantage of the girl. She was a willing partner during their sexual malpractices.

'I refuse to help any more!' I announced firmly.

'But Emmeline only wanted to meet you.'

'Yes,' she said. 'We have to go now, anyway. For another session.'

'Stop off at the Chapel on your way!' I urged. 'Kneel down and pray for guidance.'

'We have all the guidance we need,' replied Neil with a bovine grin. 'Thanks to Emmeline. She keeps us straight.'

'*Us*? It isn't just you, Neil?'

'No. She cracks the whip over eight of us.'

'Eight!' I stared at her in amazement. 'How ever do you manage it?'

'I use a megaphone.'

'This has got to stop!' I yelled.

'It can't, old chap,' said Neil. 'Practice makes perfect.'

'The eight of them depend on me,' said Emmeline.

'But it's indecent!' I bellowed.

'It's exhausting,' conceded Neil. 'I know that. But it leaves you with a tremendous feeling of satisfaction. Well, you must have tried it yourself, Christopher.'

'I haven't!'

'But I'm sure you'd be good at it,' noted Emmeline. 'You've got such a powerful body.'

Neil smiled fondly at her. 'You'll have to take him in hand.'

'I'd love to,' she said. 'Don't be frightened about starting from scratch. I was a complete beginner when I came up to Oxford. It was Alf Ord who taught me.'

'Alf Ord?' I repeated.

'I wanted to work with the best cox.'

I had heard enough. Standing up, I ushered them both to the door and told them that I could spare them no more time. Emmeline really was very short. As I stared down at her, a frightening thought hit me. Eight young men every afternoon had taken their toll of her. She had probably arrived at Oxford as a strapping girl of six feet and been steadily eroded by regular octagonal sex.

'I'm sorry,' I said, 'but I strongly disapprove of it!'

'Does that mean you won't be there to cheer us on in the Boat Race?' she asked with patent disappointment. 'I may never get to cox the crew again.'

'Come on, Emmeline,' said Neil. 'Mustn't keep Alf waiting.' He turned to me. 'Alf is our coach. He coxed the Oxford crew twenty years ago. They never lost when he was in charge.'

He escorted her out and I took the egg off my face.

If my fellow-undergraduates now took a different view of me, they also did so of Ferriday. During Michaelmas Term, he had been a retiring type with a habit of retiring every so often: in Hilary Term, he had taken on a new identity and it was one I did not recognize.

'Where's P.C. Ferriday this morning?'

'You're brave to share tutorials with him, Mountjoy?'

'How many ten minutes in twenty-four hours?'

'Ask P.C. Ferriday.'

Boisterous laughter in the beer cellar. I could not make head or tail of it. Everybody was in on the joke except me. And possibly Ferriday himself. I decided to find out and invited him to coffee in my room. It was an occasion for treading warily.

'Have you ever thought about reading Law?' I said.

'I've thought about reading anything but FTI.' he moaned. 'Let's face it, Mountjoy, we'd get more education reading an eye-chart.'

'Depends,' I said sagely.

'On what?'

'On what you want to do with your future. In some walks of life, Forestry, Theology and Industrial Archeology could be an asset.'

'Name one!' he challenged.

'I can't, offhand,' I confessed, 'unless you want to be a religious gamekeeper with an interest in Victorian sprockets.' I used my friendliest voice. 'What *do* you want to be, old chap?'

'You'd only laugh.'

'Of course, I wouldn't.'

'It's such an absurd ambition, really.'

'I've guessed. You want to be an actor.'

He nodded. Even after the traumas of *King Lear*, he was still wedded to the theatre. It was the only place he felt safe. He was, however, a realist.

'I could never make a living at it.'

'There are other professions where you could use your acting ability,' I reminded him. 'The Church, for instance.'

'I never want to swing another bloody incense-burner!'

'Teaching?'

'I'm too shy.'

'Public relations?'

'I'm too honest.'

'Auctioneering? Selling cars? Bingo-calling?'

'What are you driving at, Mountjoy?'

'The Law,' I said. 'You'd make a terrific barrister. On the other hand, you might find it more rewarding to be a humble bobby on the beat. Tell me, Ferriday, have you ever considered becoming a police constable?'

'And I thought you were my friend!' he wailed.

Close to tears, he rushed out. Chiding myself for my stupidity, I went to his room to apologize but he was not there. I recalled what Bernard had said about Ferriday's room-mates but there were none. I took a peep into his bedroom and saw what my scout had meant.

Sellotaped to the walls, were coloured posters of muscle men showing off their bulges with uninhibited pride. I was still in the dark. Why was he P.C. Ferriday? Were these dear gentlemen in their natty trunks all off-duty policemen?

It was midnight before I found out. A well-known time for secrets.

'Can I come in, Mountjoy?' he asked.

'Yes, I was only reading before sloping off to my pit.'

'I came to say sorry. For rushing off like that.'

'It was my fault, Ferriday. I was crass.'

We traded apologies and then I made him a coffee. Eventually, he got round to it, staring at the carpet and talking in an undertone.

'You've heard, haven't you?'

'Yes.'

'P.C. doesn't stand for Police Constable.'

'Privy Councillor?'

'No. It stands for – Portnoy's Complaint.'

'My dear chap, that's awful!' I sympathized. 'I just didn't know you were ill. Is it like . . . Parkinson's Disease?'

'*Portnoy's Complaint* is a book.'

'I don't see why you should be so guilt-stricken about having a book. I've got whole shelves of them.'

'Portnoy is the central character. He's . . . me!'

In halting language, he forced out the explanation.

Ferriday was wrong. It sounded as if Portnoy was a raw novice compared with him. He was methodical and had got it down to an exact ten minutes. It was compulsive and occurred in all sorts of places.

His public disgrace had arisen at the college. As he crossed from one building to another by means of the charming Venetian-style bridge that connected them, he was seduced by the large wood-carving of an Italian saint holding a circle of flame. While Ferriday was entering the burning orifice, a couple of undergraduates happened to walk down below and overhear him.

The structure was now known as the Bridge of Sighs.

It got worse the more I listened. Innocent objects took on a whole new dimension for me. I would never be able to look at the pocket of a fur coat again without thinking of that poor, unsuspecting woman who stood next to Ferriday on a crowded tube train between Goodge Street and East Finchley.

'Then there was that time in the British Museum,' he confessed. 'In a hollowed-out copy of *Pilgrim's Progress*. I hate to think what the next borrower must have suffered.'

'It's got to stop, Ferriday.'

'I know. I'm at a crisis stage now. FTI is to blame. If I wasn't studying Forestry and going to Christ Almighty! Meadows every day, it would never have happened.'

'What?'

'I've fallen in love with a copper beech.'

He had finally found the courage to talk about his problem and he had turned to me for help. I was touched. I sought to get at the roots of his condition.

'Don't women attract you at all?' I asked. 'And I don't just mean those who wear fur coats on the London Underground.'

'Yes, they do. But only a certain sort of woman.'

'Such as?'

'Boadicea. Catherine the Great. Lucrezia Borgia.'

I think I got his number fairly accurately.

'You won't find many women like that in Oxford, I'm afraid.'

'Even if I did, they wouldn't look twice at me. I go to pieces in female company. Not like you.' His voice became a hushed whisper. 'Who was the first woman?'

'Eve.'

'No – *your* first woman!'

'Look here, Ferriday – '

'Come on. I've bared my soul to you,' he reasoned. 'Own up. When did you first see a mature woman naked?'

'At Eton. She was the housemaster's wife.'

'Did she apprentice you to sexual pleasure?'

'Not exactly – but I was sort of indentured.'

'That's the kind of woman for me!' he asserted. 'One who'll take me by the scruff of the neck and sort me out. Help me to find such a woman, Mountjoy. Save me. Please!'

'I'll do what I can,' I promised. 'On one condition!'

'What's that?'

'Woodman, spare that tree . . . '

'I'll break off our engagement tomorrow!'

Ferriday went off to his room a happier person. The two hours spent with me might make all the difference to the ten minutes he spent alone. There *had* to be a woman for him. Someone in the Boadicea mould. An imperious virago who drove into his life with knives on her wheels. A queen of her sex who took him by sovereignty of nature. A she-warrior who stormed the castle of his sexual problems and left it a smoking ruin.

Where could I possibly find such a creature?

Unknown to me, she was lying on my desk at that moment.

Her name was Roxanne Doggerel.

Chapter Ten: POETRY IN MOTION

When Davinia made up her mind to do something, it was virtually impossible to prevent her from doing it. I wrote to tell her that it would not be convenient for her to visit me and I gave her ten good reasons why she would be wasting her time in coming to Oxford but she ignored it all. On the day appointed and at the hour stipulated, she knocked on my door and sailed in.

'What a pokey little college!' she sneered.

'I like it.'

'Little things please little minds.'

'If you're going to be rude about Corpus Delicti – '

'Make me some tea, Christopher,' she ordered with a wave of her hand. 'Unless you have a real drink to offer me.'

'I'll put the kettle on.'

While I made the tea and got out some cake and biscuits, Davinia did a tour of my room and inspected all my books and belongings. She was not impressed with her findings.

'It doesn't look like the study of a superman.'

'A what?'

'No need to be modest, Christopher. I know what happened in that play. I saw the review in *The Times*. You're famous. You can't hide Great Aunt Lucy under a bushel now.'

'Have some cake,' I said, thrusting it at her.

'No thank you. I'm on a diet.'

'Are you?'

'Yes. I only eat young men between meals.'

Over a cup of tea, she continued to tease and bait me until I realized the true purpose of her visit. She was jealous. My rise to spectacular prominence at Oxford had excited her envy and brought out her competitive streak. Like a true Mountjoy, Davinia had the urge to be first.

'Mother told me about your engagement,' I remarked.

'Which engagement?'

'The mountaineer.'

'Which one? I was engaged to three different mountaineers. When I was in Switzerland, I had mountaineers climbing all over me.'

'Are you engaged at the moment?'

'Loosely. I've agreed to wear his ring until his wife finds out about me.' She reclined on my sofa. 'But what about you? I expected you to be besieged by girls. With a reputation like yours, they ought to be trying to break down your door.'

'Sarcasm is the lowest form of wit, Davinia.'

'That's why I knew you'd be able to appreciate it.'

We continued to spat for another quarter of an hour and then there was a knock on the door. Emmeline Partridge came in with Neil Blythe.

'Oh, sorry to interrupt you,' said Emmeline, disappointed. 'I didn't realize that you had company.'

'This is my sister,' I introduced. 'Davinia.'

Emmeline brightened when she saw that I was not entertaining a girlfriend. Neil, meanwhile, had gone weak at the knees. When I overlooked the catalogue of her faults and crimes, I had to admit that my sister was a very attractive and sophisticated young woman. Davinia certainly knew how to use her charms.

'I do so like strong and handsome men!' she announced.

'Neil is a rowing Blue,' I said. 'He strokes for the Oxford crew.'

'He can stroke for me any time that he wishes.'

'Thank you!' replied Neil, all grin and gullibility.

'Do you have a room in the college?' Davinia asked.

'Yes. I'm at the top of Staircase One.'

'How appropriate, Neil! I'd love to see it!' She flashed him a smile that made him blush to his socks. 'And I'd love to see your room as well. Will you show it to me?'

'Behave yourself, Davinia,' I warned. 'Neil is in training for the Boat Race.'

'I like them when they're fit and supple!'

'You can't see my room from here,' Neil said helpfully, 'but we'd probably get a glimpse of it from the bedroom.'

'Say no more, darling!'

Davinia had taken him by the hand and whisked him into the bedroom before he knew what hit him. I shrugged apologetically at Emmeline. Alone with me for the first time, she gave me the adoring look with which I was becoming all too familiar. If Neil had fallen for one member of the Mountjoy family, she had fallen for another. Emmeline Partridge was an amorous cox who wanted to whisper sweet nothings into my ear through her megaphone.

'I just called in to ask you a favour, Christopher.'

'Ask away.'

'Will you come and watch us practice some time, please?'

'Well – '

'Oh, do promise that you will! I'd be able to cox so much better with you on the riverbank cheering us on. I'm sure you'd like to do your bit towards helping Oxford to win.'

'Put like that, how can I refuse?' I said.

'Thank you, thank you!' She was wagging her tail furiously.

'More power to your elbow, Emmeline. It must be difficult for you, being the only woman in a boat full of men.'

'I like it. Marvellous to be able to fly the flag!'

'Flag?'

'Women's Lib. Slowly but surely, we're breaking into all the male bastions at Oxford. OUDS, the Union, the Boat Race . . . '

'Yes,' I added flippantly, 'they'll be letting you into the Gents at the Randolph next.'

'We've been kept out too long!'

'I shouldn't worry. It's not much to write home about.'

'Kept out from positions of power and influence.' She relaxed and gave me her little smile. 'I'm sorry. I didn't mean to get on my soapbox. But it is important to me. That's why I'm helping in the campaign.'

'Campaign?'

'To get a woman elected as Professor of Poetry. It would be a fantastic achievement if we brought it off. And she'd make as good a Professor as any of the men standing.'

'She?' I had shown only a cursory interest in the forthcoming election of a new Professor. 'Who might she be?'

'Roxanne Doggerel.'

The name sounded familiar somehow. I tried to think why.

'She'd be glad of your support if you felt able to give it, Christopher,' said Emmeline seriously. 'To have someone like *you* on the feminist bandwagon! Wow! That would be terrific!'

I was about to answer when a sixth sense took my attention elsewhere. Conversation in the bedroom had stopped. There was a long ominous silence and then it was broken by light moaning noises from the throat of our resident oarsman. Emmeline and I darted into the bedroom together.

Davinia and Neil were standing side by side and looking out of the bedroom window. Nothing seemed to be amiss until I got right up to them and saw that she had her hand deep in his trouser pocket.

'Stop it!' I shouted.

Cut off in mid-moan, Neil jumped guiltily away from my sister. Davinia was in no way perturbed and looked as if she might have been interrupted while in the act of stirring her tea.

'We were *so* enjoying the view of Neil's bedroom!'

Emmeline now took over. Shocked at the thought that one of her crew might have his manly marrow sapped in broad daylight, she stepped up to him with eyes blazing.

'Have you forgotten our practice this afternoon?'
'No, Emmeline.'
'And our rules about . . . *that* sort of thing?'
'No, Emmeline.'
'Then get down to the river at once!' He shot Davinia a furtive glance. 'At once, Neil!'
'Yes, Emmeline,' he said and went meekly out.
'As for you, Miss Mountjoy,' continued the cox, rounding on Davinia, 'I'll thank you to keep your hands off my crew. They need all the strength they have for their rowing!'
'Such a waste of prime English beef, darling!' opined Davinia.
'The Boat Race comes first!' insisted Emmeline. 'Until that is over, the whole eight has had to make the supreme sacrifice!' She turned to me. 'Goodbye, Christopher,' she said and stalked out.
I admired her spirit and vitality. Emmeline Partridge was game.
'Time for you to go, I think, Davinia.'
'Don't you have any more tasty young men dropping in?'
'Not while you're here.'
'I'll be back,' she threatened.
'You won't be made welcome.'
'Not by you, maybe. But something tells me I might get a tickertape reception elsewhere.' She went into the other room. 'Goodbye . . .'
'Goodbye and good riddance!'
'Compliments pass when the quality meet.'
'I'll see you down to the lodge,' I said, leading the way. 'I'd like to be quite certain you leave the premises.'
'How do I get to the river?' she asked casually.
'By catching the next train out of here!'
'I knew you'd enjoy your sister's visit . . .'
When I had shown her out into Merkin Lane and wallowed in recrimination for a while, I went back up to my room to conduct a search. When Emmeline had mentioned a name, I felt sure that I had seen it on a piece of paper

somewhere and so I sifted through the mounds of correspondence on my desk. It was in a pile that was waiting to be bagged up for incineration by Bernard.

Roxanne Doggerel had addressed me in lilting verse.

Mr Mountjoy, burning bright,
Come and set my cause alight.
Work for me with heart and hand,
Let your codpiece make a stand
For freedom, truth and old Roxanne.
(PS I'm staying at The Flying Swan.)
(PPS Come and find me there
And help me sit down in that Chair.)

It might not be in the Keats league but it had a pleasing rhythm and a simple integrity to which I responded at once. The very least I could do was to make contact with her and to offer my tacit support.

I decided to call on her the next day.

Bernard was in a cheerful mood when he bounced into my bedroom on the following morning. He went through his rituals with a spring in his step and scattered anecdotes from below stairs all over me. I did not *intend* to rob him of his good humour.

'Where exactly is The Flying Swan?' I asked innocently.

He was shocked. '*You* are going there, Mr Mountjoy?'

'To see a woman.'

'I am well aware of why people visit that establishment,' he said meaningfully. 'I beg you to ask yourself some questions first: is it wise?'

'Wise?'

'Is it healthy?'

'Healthy?'

'And is it really necessary?'

'Do I gather that you're against the idea, Bernard?'

'My young gentlemen do not frequent The Flying Swan.'

'I wasn't going to frequent it. Just pop in there once.'

'Once is more than enough!'

'In that case, I'll invite her here.'

'Mr Mountjoy!' He had his matches out in a flash. 'I simply could not permit that in one of my rooms.'

'But I want to meet her. She's different to the others.'

'Them women is all the same, sir!'

'Not Roxanne. She does it in verse.'

I could see his brain trying to comprehend this new perversion.

'Forget those women!' he urged. 'Stay among your male friends here.'

'But I'm told she'd be every bit as good at it as a man.'

'Fight against it, sir!'

'I'm attracted by her rhythm.'

'Mr Mount . . . joy!'

'And her couplets.'

He croaked helplessly. I tried to assuage his fears by showing him Roxanne's poems but he read a significance into the lines that scandalized him even more.

'Forswear this painted lady, sir!'

'She doesn't want money from me, Bernard.'

'We both know what she wants!'

'She'd like my full weight behind her, that's all.'

'It shouldn't be *allowed*, sir!'

'But I have great sympathy for what she's trying to do.' I saw his jaw sag. 'Roxanne wants to get at male bastions.' His eyes filmed over. 'For heaven's sake, Bernard, what's *wrong* with having a woman in professorial robes?'

'My young gentlemen don't do such things!' he howled.

And sweeping up the bagged correspondence, he went off to start a fire that would burn out its accumulated sin. When I later peeped through my window, he was sending up smoke signals to the Almighty, requesting a medium-sized thunderbolt for The Flying Swan.

Corpus Delicti would not have been the same without Bernard.

To call it a spit and sawdust pub would be to exaggerate its charms. The Flying Swan was earthbound in every sense. Dark, filthy and labyrinthine, it smelled in equal parts of stale beer and unspecified wickedness. Drunken men made raucous comments, bold, bare-breasted women lolled in corners, the barmaid was a Cockney hermaphrodite and the landlord carried a sawn-off shotgun.

Ideal habitat for a future Professor of Poetry.

There was even a chair.

Roxanne Doggerel looked completely at home. Large, boisterous, motherly and voluptuous, she might have been Mistress Quickly doing an impression of Irma La Douce. The slit skirt and the donkey jacket did not at first accord with my notion of a poet but they grew on me as a winning combination. So did Roxanne's breasts. They were twin hillocks of undulating loveliness.

Her big, open, cheerful face spurned cosmetics and relied on its own deep natural colouring. The blue eyes were whirlpools of joyous experience. The full lips were parted to reveal white, attractively uneven teeth. There was a sense of optimism about her double chin. She wore long, vulgar earrings and a necklace made up of wooden balls the size of walnuts.

The sense of womanhood and vitality and raw power was almost overwhelming. Roxanne Doggerel was an Earth Mother with an interest in versification. She generated warmth and sexuality and goodwill.

Her personality washed over me like warm waves.

'Chris!' She crushed my fingers in a handshake. 'You came!'

The announcement produced grunts from competitors in the gloom.

'I wanted to thank you for your poem,' I said.

'That's nothing, darling! I've written three dozen more since that one. I'm into free verse at the moment.' She guffawed. 'But only because no bugger will pay me for it.'

She had Nanny Groat's uncomplicated directness and I liked her.

'What do you think your chances are, Roxanne?'

'When I started – none at all.'

'And now?'

'We've started to roll, Chris. The show is on the road. I've built up a lot of support since I linked up with Oxford United.'

'As a player?' It was by no means an absurd question. She would have made a formidable central defender. 'What's your position?'

'Left out,' she said and guffawed again. 'No, I come into my own at half-time. Over the public address system.'

'They let you recite your poems?'

'No,' she said, 'but I read out the half-time scores in rhyming couplets. The spectators seem to like it. They haven't nailed a referee to the goalposts for weeks.'

She called for two pints of beer and began to sip them both.

'What's the next stage?' I asked.

'To flush the other candidates out into the open. At the moment, they're all hiding from me.'

I was not surprised. She would have intimidated Shelley.

'Join my campaign, Chris. Your support is vital.'

'But I don't even have a vote,' I pointed out. 'The Professor of Poetry is elected by the Senior Members of the University.'

'They'd take notice of you, though.'

'I doubt it, Roxanne.'

'They would!' She hitched up her skirt to reveal a fleshy thigh encased in gold lamé. 'Let me give it to you straight, Chris. I want your name!'

'But it wouldn't suit you.'

She rocked with mirth and pummelled my back. 'I need your name for publicity purposes,' she explained. 'Do I get it?'

'Well, I suppose so . . . '

'You've got reservations about me?'

'The truth is that I don't really know much about you, Roxanne. Or your poetry.'

'We'll soon put that right. Know how to make instant coffee?'

'Of course.'

'Well, I have the knack of making Instant Poetry.'

And she told me her story in glorious technicolour.

Roxanne Doggerel was no sensitive soul who locked herself away and waited for the inspiration that would allow her to deliver a slim volume of verse to Faber and Faber every nine years. She believed in mass production.

It was while she was working as a riveter in a Coventry car factory that she discovered her gift and she had been turning out the stuff at an alarming rate ever since. Having abandoned her husband and the man she was living with, she devoted herself to full-time writing and felt, at forty, that she was at last on the verge of making it into the great anthology of fame.

'I started on the back of matchboxes,' she admitted.

'That's one way to set the Thames on fire.'

'Then I moved on to greetings cards.'

'What was your big break?' I wondered.

'Someone gave me a can of aerosol paint so I versified three blocks of flats and a double decker bus. It got me noticed.'

To demonstrate her creative technique, Roxanne produced some poems there and then on subjects of my own choice. It was like watching spontaneous combustion. Here was a woman who would grace the Chair of Poetry.

'And there's one more reason why I should get it,' she argued. 'The Professorship is a titular appointment and nobody can touch me when it comes to tits!'

'I'm with you, Roxanne!' I said happily.

'That's great, Chris!'

'Just tell me what to do.'

'You've already done it, sweetheart.'

She gave me a kiss that left me vibrating for days.

When Gordy Hollis rang to tell me that he would be coming to Oxford for an interview, I was thrilled. When he added that Rosemary Anne would be coming as well because it was her half-term, I was beside myself with joy. But when he told me that Carlotta Nashe would be in tow as well, I began to have misgivings. My fears were justified.

I bought sandwiches and cakes to give them all a splendid tea and then changed into my tracksuit to convey athletic nonchalance. As I waited for them to arrive, I prayed that Rosemary Anne would somehow come first and alone. When there was a knock on the door, I leapt to fling it open.

'Have you found her yet?' It was Ferriday. 'Well?'

'Give me time.'

'But I need salvation, Mountjoy. Where's my Boadicea?'

'I'm working on it,' I assured him. 'Are you behaving?'

'Oh yes. I'm abiding by the Monroe Doctrine. Hands off!'

'What about that copper beech?'

'I'm learning to live without it.'

'Well done, Ferriday! You made the right decision. We had a boy at Eton who had an affair with a tree. It had dire consequences.'

'Did he get the clap?'

'Worse. He had a nasty dose of Dutch Elm Disease.' I eased him off down the stairs. 'You just hold on for a bit and your Boadicea will come.'

Half an hour passed before I heard more steps on the staircase. A female tread. It had to be Rosemary Anne this time. I threw the door open once more to find Carlotta Nashe supporting herself against the wall. My disappointment changed to compassion at once.

'What's the matter?'

'I feel awful, Christopher,' she said as I helped her in. 'Hot flushes, pain in the stomach and a pounding headache. Do you think I could possibly lie down for a bit?'

'Yes, yes. Come in here . . . '

I took her into the bedroom and lowered her gently on to the bed.

'Have you got an aspirin or something, please?'

'In the bathroom. They're soluble.'

'Perfect . . . '

Leaving her in agony on the bed, I went into the

bathroom and got the aspirins from the cabinet. They dissolved slowly in the water then I took the glass through to her. She was now in bed under the sheets with her eyes closed. Putting the glass down, I bent close to see if she had fallen asleep. A hand shot out to grip my wrist.

'Come and join me!' she yelled.

The invalid had made an astonishing recovery. She hurled back the sheets to show that she was completely naked and pulled me on top of her. When I surfaced from the first kiss, I gasped a protest.

'Carlotta! You must be mad!'

'I am. Sex-mad!'

'The others might come!'

'Not before we do.' She pulled down the trousers of my track suit. 'I need a quickie.'

'I've just brought you a soluble aspirin.'

'Give me *this*!' she commanded as her hands found me.

Another kiss stopped my mouth and put an end to any resistance. Carlotta had learned a great deal since our last meeting. This was no frantic roll in the hay-loft while fully-clothed. She now knew that there was much more to it than that. After a dry run-through with me, she now wanted a full performance. So did I.

The warmth of her body and the urgency of her passion made me lengthen at once. She twisted and turned then pulled me forward by the hips. With a fluke thrust, I suddenly entered a moist, receptive cavern of delight. It was wonderful. Carlotta agreed. The moment that I achieved full penetration, she went off like a firework display, screaming, moaning, sucking, biting and digging her fingernails into me.

As the pyrotechnics were ending and I was getting ready for my turn with the blue touchpaper, there was a knock on the door in the other room. I was off her in a split second.

'Christopher?' It was Gordy's voice.

'I'll be out in a second!' I called.

'Where are you?'

'In the bathroom!'

'Have you seen Carlotta?'

'Not recently,' I said, looking down at her nude and sated body.

'But I'm sure she was on her way here.'

Carlotta had now come out of her post-coital daze and was trying to beckon me over for a second helping. I signalled wildly to her that we had company and that she should get dressed. She laughed.

'What was that?' demanded Gordy.

'Me,' I replied, hauling up my track suit trousers and trying to mimic the laugh. 'I hit my funny bone on the wash basin.'

'Can I come in?'

'No!' I exclaimed as the door inched open. 'I'm coming out.'

I joined him in the other room and closed the bedroom door firmly behind me. With an effort, I manufactured a smile of interest.

'How did the interview go?'

'Fine. But I'm more worried about Carlotta at the moment.'

'So am I.'

'She's so impulsive.'

'Yes, I'd go along with that description of her.'

'We were in the High Street together and she suddenly charged off. I wondered if she'd got here before me. Carlotta promised we'd meet here if we got parted.'

'She must have got lost in the college somewhere, Gordy,' I said, shepherding him towards the door. 'Why not go and search for her?'

'But you're the one who knows his way around, Christopher. You go and look for her while I stay here.'

'Carlotta would much rather be found by you.'

His guileless face coloured. 'You're right. Where shall I go?'

'Everywhere.'

As soon as he had left, I tore back into the bedroom.

'For God's sake, Carlotta! Put your clothes on!'

'Afterwards.'

'Gordy's on the prowl. He's looking for you.'

'Come back to bed,' she insisted, leaping up to take hold of me. 'I'm ready for more. Now . . .'

She was dragging me across the room when we heard another knock on the outer door. Rosemary Anne entered and called out to me.

'Christopher? Are you there?'

I shed Carlotta, hissed at her to put her clothes on then shot into the other room. Rosemary Anne looked so beautiful and pleased to see me that my guilt whirred away like an electric fan. She stepped forward and kissed me on the cheek.

'Your face is hot, Christopher,' she said with concern.

'It's the excitement,' I explained. 'Gordy has gone to search for Carlotta.'

'Yes, I just met him on the stairs. I told him not to hurry.'

'What?'

'I thought you'd appreciate some time alone with me.'

'Yes!' I remembered Carlotta. 'No!' I saw her face cloud. 'Could I just settle for maybe?'

'What kind of a welcome is that?' she complained.

'Look, I'm sorry, Rosemary Anne,' I said, lowering my voice to a whisper. 'Are you sure you wouldn't like me to show you around the college?'

'I came to see *you*.'

'Then you'll have to walk sideways.'

'Don't you understand, you silly boy?' she said with a laugh. 'I want some time alone with you. In private.' She glanced towards the door. 'Can you lock that?'

'No. But I sometimes sport my oak.'

'I was rather hoping you would.'

'My oak is the outer door, Rosemary Anne.'

'Then let's sport it,' she decided and ran to do the necessary. We moved to the sofa. 'Such a long time since we last met!'

'Yes, I must apologize for what happened at the flat.'

'You weren't to know that Davinia was there.' She raised

an eyebrow. 'There's nobody in your bed now, though, is there?'

'No . . . Yes! . . . I mean . . . '

'Christopher, what *is* the matter with you?'

'Gordy will be back soon.'

'I said that we'd meet him in the lodge.'

'Carlotta might – '

'Carlotta would never dream of coming up here on her own. She's far too shy. Besides, she hardly knows you.'

'I wouldn't say that!' I murmured.

'She only bumped into you that once at our house.'

I tried to cover my confusion with words but she drowned them with her lips. I went under willingly. For those long, luscious minutes of unadulterated joy in Rosemary Anne's arms, nothing else mattered. I forgot everything else as love and lust finally had a chance to work together as a team. Entwined on the sofa, we kissed away the months of separation until we approached the point of no return. Rosemary Anne suddenly leapt up and pulled me towards the bedroom.

'Let's do it in here!'

'Rosemary Anne – no!'

But I was too late. She hurled the bedroom door open and barged straight in. I tensed myself for a shock that never came. Carlotta was not there. The open window showed that she had found herself an emergency exit. I was at last alone in a room with a bed with the girl I loved. I took her in my arms with renewed passion.

'Christopher!' Ferriday was banging on my oak.

'What the hell do you want?' I yelled, running to stop him as he opened both doors. 'I'm busy!'

'I've seen two gorgeous girls coming up here!' he panted, his eyes on stalks. 'Which one is mine?'

'Get out!'

I slammed both doors behind him and returned to the bedroom.

Rosemary Anne was against the far wall with a serene smile. Our moment had come at last. Soft music seemed to play and we moved towards each other in slow motion like figures in some erotic ballet of our own devising. When we touched, an electric current ran through me. When we kissed, its voltage intensified. When we sank gracefully to the bed, a clanging sound started inside my head. As I lay on top of her and felt my body against hers, the clanging got louder and louder until I realized what it was.

The bell that signalled the end of visiting hours.

'Take me, Christopher!' she whispered. 'Take me!'

But it was too late. Before I could make another move, I heard yet another flurry of door-opening then Bernard's voice spoke from the other room.

'I will be coming in to make that bed in a moment, sir!'

There was no answer to that.

Chapter Eleven:
WINNING AND LOSING

Roxanne Doggerel wasted no time at all in bringing my name into play as a campaign weapon. When the headline MOUNTJOY PREFERS DOGGEREL appeared in the newspapers, the response was immediate. Crowds of helpers came to swell her election headquarters and the landlord of The Flying Swan had to take on five new barmaids and a bigger shotgun. Letters of encouragement came in from Senior Members all over the country. Donations flooded in to boost her fighting fund and her morale. She was still a long way from winning, but we had made distinct progress.

The Professorship was a four-cornered contest.

Roxanne's opponent in Oxford itself was none other than Lance Arundel who was desperate to restore his credibility after the OUDS fiasco. It was true that he had never actually written any poetry but he did have the distinction of having proved that Shakespeare's sonnets were written by Sir Isaac Newton (and that, conversely, the Law of Gravity had been discovered during a nocturnal tryst in an orchard with the Dark Lady).

D.H. Lawrence was an altogether faster horse in the race. He was not really D.H. Lawrence but was sent to bear witness of D.H. Lawrence. Friends advised him to change his name to avoid confusion but he refused and continued to turn out poetry that bore a striking similarity to that of his namesake. His best poem was a reworking in verse of the Master's most notorious novel and I had to concede that it had a certain verve and excitement.

I have heard, latterly,

That Sir Clifford Chatterley
Has taken up philately,
And has something to lick at last.

Fortunately, D.H. Lawrence torpedoed his own chances. Roxanne came waddling over to me at The Flying Swan one day to pass on the glad tidings.

'Great news, Chris! D.H. Lawrence is dead.'

'I know that. He turned up his toes in 1930.'

'Not the *real* D.H. Lawrence,' she said. 'The fake D.H. Lawrence.'

'He died?'

'Effectively. It wasn't his real name, you see.'

'What was?'

'Gerard Manley Hopkins.'

'How do you know?'

'His ex-wife spilled the beans on the bugger. She got fed up with being sent his crappy poems instead of maintenance payments.' She hugged me tight. 'He's lost his following, Chris! Even the Gamekeepers' Association has withdrawn its support.'

I could understand why. Changing from Gerard Manley to David Herbert had been a tactical error. That he should trade religious inspiration for grunts and groans in Nottinghamshire upset the purists completely. Had he kept his real name, he could have bounced into the Chair on sprung rhythm.

'One down, two to go!' I observed.

'Lance Arundel has dropped out as well!' she said with a guffaw. 'I put paid to him in that telly interview.'

'What did you say, Roxanne?'

'I told him that he already *was* a Professor and that he shouldn't be so bloody greedy. If he held two Chairs, I said, he'd be after a sodding Table next. Even the interviewer laughed at him.'

'So there's only two of you left in the hunt.'

'Yes. Roxanne Doggerel and W.H. Hauden-Smith!'

'He won't be easy to beat,' I admitted.

'If only the old turd would come out and fight!' she

complained. 'I bet I could wipe the floor with him in public debate!'

'You could wipe the floor with Frank Bruno,' I noted.

'What sort of poetry does *he* write?'

'Coming back to W.H. Hauden-Smith . . . '

He was the clear favourite to win. The most renowned and prolific poet in the Western hemisphere, W.H. Hauden-Smith had become a legend in his own very long lifetime. He now lived in hermetic isolation in Ibiza visited only by local peasants and by the occasional coach party from Thomson Holidays. The sheer impenetrability of his work meant that it was taken very seriously and it had been translated into fifty-seven different languages – including English.

'You have to hand it to him,' conceded Roxanne. 'His poetry has actually got better in recent years.'

'I know. And he's still churning it out at ninety!'

'I'll still be doing it when I'm that age!' she boasted with a chuckle. 'And I'll still be writing poetry as well. In fact, I'll probably have worked out by then how to do both at the same time!'

'As long as you don't underestimate Hauden-Smith,' I warned.

'I won't, sweetheart,' she promised. 'Besides, whatever happens, I've had the time of my little life in this election. It's been bloody marvellous, Chris. Thanks to people like you.'

'I've done nothing.'

'Yes, you did. You're my Beefcake Factor. Because of you, every woman with a vote wants to give it to me.'

'Emmeline is the person to thank,' I reminded her. 'She was the one who first got me interested in your cause.'

She grinned wickedly. 'I'll leave *you* to thank her, Chris.'

'What do you mean?'

'You'll find out. Em will expect to collect her dues.'

The Flying Swan suddenly hit an air pocket.

I have always found the rowing fraternity a rather rum lot. Hearty fellows with huge hands and thick thighs who all but murder themselves for the sole purpose of travelling backwards at speed over water when a bicycle ride along the towpath would get them there just as quickly and with much more comfort. Somehow I am out of sympathy with their objectives.

Perhaps I sang the Eton Boating Song once too often.

My reservations about the sport lapped at my mind again as I watched the Oxford crew in practice on the Isis. They moved with fluency and coordination, urged on by Emmeline Partridge through her monster megaphone. Galley slaves to the lash of her tongue, the eight of them heaved on their oars for all they were worth. Neil Blythe, glistening with perspiration and noble endeavour, set a punishing pace for the others to follow.

When it was all over, I stood on the steps of the boathouse with the delighted cox. The crew remained in the boat to get their breath back and to wait for the strength to lift their craft ashore.

'What did you think, Christopher?' asked Emmeline.

'You were terrific!' I congratulated.

'I'm sure we can do it on the day!' she argued then her features darkened. 'If we get no distractions.'

'Distractions?'

'Didn't you know? She's been back.'

'Who?'

'Your sister.'

'When?'

'Two or three times.'

'Why didn't she tell me that she was in Oxford?'

'Because she didn't come to see you, Christopher.'

Even as Emmeline said that, a familiar figure appeared on the opposite bank. Davinia was wearing a white fur coat, tight black corduroy trousers and a pair of thigh-length red boots. When Neil Blythe saw her, his face lit up like the Blackpool Illuminations. He was not the only spellbound oarsman. As Davinia waved across the water, eight exhausted young men sat up smartly in their boat and waved back in unison.

'It's getting to be a problem,' confided Emmeline.

'I'll speak to her.'

'It's so unfair. To put temptation in their way. And it's not as if they are the only ones who have had to restrain themselves.'

'I don't follow.'

'Me, Christopher. As cox, I've tried to set an example.' Her eyes searched mine. 'Self-denial can be very painful.'

'But good for the soul.'

'Good for the Boat Race as well. That's why we do it.'

'Or don't do it, as the case might be.'

She took my hand. 'Could I ask you for a rather special favour?' My hesitation was obvious. 'You'd be helping Oxford to win,' she pointed out. 'Please.'

'What do you want me to do?'

'Stand near the finishing line. I'll get you a place on a boat that will be moored there.' She gave me a radiant smile. 'If I saw you as we rowed over the final couple of hundred yards, I'm sure it would inspire me to get more out of my crew.'

'Well, I suppose I could be there . . . '

'Oh, thank you, Christopher!' she said, grabbing my lapels so that she could hoist herself up to kiss me on the chin. 'It will make all the difference to me.'

I looked at Davinia who was still holding the eight enthralled.

'Would you like me to get my sister on that boat as well?'

'Why?'

'If I inspire you, she might inspire *them*,' I suggested. 'Don't you think that Neil Blythe would pull a little harder on his oar if he knew who was waiting at the finishing line.'

'It might just work!' she agreed.

'They're the donkeys: Davinia is the carrot.'

'As long as they don't get a bite before the race itself,' she insisted. 'That would ruin everything.'

'Leave it to me, Emmeline. I'll have a stern word with my sister.'

'Will she do as you ask?'

'No. But she'll do as I *tell* her. That's a promise.'

It was also wishful thinking. Davinia had never done what I or anyone else had told her. She was a law unto herself and it was a mistake to think that even such an important event as a Boat Race could interfere with her habit of self-legislation.

On the day of the election for the Professorship, we set up a large dais outside the Radcliffe Camera Shop so that Roxanne Doggerel could declaim her poetry to the vast audience that had gathered there. I was kept busy signing autographs on her behalf and she did not mind in the slightest that my queue of women was twice as long as her queue of men. While my admirers only got a name, however, hers got an instant poem in their autograph books.

'It's a fantastic turn-out, Roxanne!' I said.

'I can't get over it, Chris! And look how many Oxford United fans are here. I'm really bloody touched by that!'

She waved at the football supporters who set up a chant.

'Roxy for Oxy! Hauden-Smith is poxy!'

'Oxford United – ten!' she shouted. 'Liverpool – nil again!'

To show their delight, they hoisted up banners with her name on them and then made a concerted charge at the police cordon. She was thrilled with them.

'If I could find a rhyme for "hooligan", I'd throw them a poem.'

'More! More! More! More!' A general chant went up.

Roxanne silenced her audience with outstretched arms then launched herself into another series of readings. It was poetry with some practical use. A mental biscuit that they could munch and enjoy there and then. Not some inedible hunk of verse locked away in the larder of some anthology for a minority palate.

Everybody was truly impressed with her performance.

'What a woman!' Ferriday was open-mouthed and overawed.

'She does have style, doesn't she?' I commented.

'What an amazing, dynamic, full-blooded creature!'

Ferriday was improving. His private life had taken a healthier direction since he had stopped writing letters to the copper beech. His mind was so preoccupied with the feminine gender now that he could hardly spare ten minutes for himself.

'Do you think she'll get elected, Mountjoy?'

'She deserves to!'

'Just *look* at her! She's magificent!'

I looked at her again and saw for the first time that – yes, maybe, in a certain way – there was a touch of Boadicea about her.

All day long the voice of Roxanne rolled. Votes were cast and then counted. Doggerel versus Hauden-Smith. The New Woman versus the silver-haired myth. The populist versus the hermit. The instant versus the everlasting.

Dead silence as the result was announced over the microphone.

'By a margin of three votes, the new Oxford Professor of Poetry is . . . '

'Good luck, Roxanne!' I whispered.

'W.H. Hauden-Smith!'

A groan of despair echoed around the dreaming spires. We had come so close to success but we had failed. All my canvassing and handshaking and autographing had been in vain. All of Roxanne's massive daily input of time and energy had gone for nothing. It was soul-destroying.

We took our disappointment back to The Flying Swan.

'We gave the old bastard a run for his money, anyway,' decided Roxanne, quaffing a pint of bitter. 'He won't forget me in a hurry.'

'You're certain to get in next time,' I encouraged.

'I'd set my heart on making it this time around,' she confessed.

We became maudlin and recriminatory. Spirits were sinking to subterranean level when a messenger burst in. It was Emmeline Partridge who brought the good news from Ibiza to Oxford.

'W.H. Hauden-Smith is null and void!'

'We know that,' said Roxanne, 'but the sod still beat me!'

'You don't understand. It's just been on the news. Hauden-Smith is dead. Apparently, he kicked the bucket eighteen years ago and nobody noticed.'

'Then who's been writing all those poems of his?' I asked.

'His constant male companion in Ibiza. It now turns out that he wrote most of the earlier stuff as well! The deception is now unmasked.' She turned to Roxanne. 'Do you realize what this means?'

'What, Em?'

'Since no Professor has ever taken up his post posthumously, then Hauden-Smith has lost by default. In other words . . . '

'I've bloody done it!' roared Roxanne.

'Yes. As soon as they've widened the Chair, you can sit in it!'

Gloom turned to jubilation and the drink flowed more freely. In the middle of her triumph, Roxanne did not forget those who had helped her. She paid glowing tributes to all her helpers and then took me to one side.

'A special thank you, Chris! You were out of this world.'

'I did what I could.'

'Without you, I'd never have done it! You were a tower of strength and I want to show my appreciation.' She pulled me so close to her that I almost vanished down the crevice between the hillocks. 'What can I do for you? Ask anything – and I do mean *anything*?'

A wild thought flashed through my mind.

Bernard was relieved that it was all over. The hordes had departed from The Flying Swan and Oxford, in his view, was a cleaner place to live in. He was glad that my personal involvement was at an end.

'That's the last you'll see of that woman, then, sir?'

'Yes, yes,' I assured him. 'Roxanne will be far too busy with her duties as Professor to bother with me.'

'That is all to the good, sir. I am very heartened when one of my young gentlemen comes back to the fold of righteousness.' He ran my bath then re-entered the bedroom. 'By the way, sir, a large parcel has arrived for you in the lodge. From a costumier!'

'Good. I was expecting it.'

'Not more play-acting, I hope?' he enquired with disapproval.

'No, no. It's not for me at all. It's for a friend.'

'I am pleased to hear it, sir. Talking of friends . . . '

Yes?'

'Mr Ferriday, sir. He seems to be on the turn.'

'I know what you're going to say, Bernard. His bedroom walls are no longer covered with bulging muscles.'

'But they are, sir. With a slight difference.'

'Difference?'

'The bulging muscles are now on female persons,' he said with distaste. 'Mr Ferriday's walls have changed their sex.'

'I'm all in favour of that!'

'You would not say so if you had to make his bed every morning, sir. I am told that it is very disconcerting to try to work in that bedroom.' He nodded his head meaningfully. 'Some of those female persons are *very* muscular, sir.'

'Where?'

'On his walls.'

Bernard went off to see to the next of his young gentlemen and to offer up a prayer that he did not look after Ferriday. If my scout had realized what I had planned for the Wykehamist, he would probably have had cardiac arrest on the spot. But what the eye does not see, the heart cannot feel and Bernard's eyes could never be allowed to see my plan in action.

It took me all morning to finalize the details and I was satisfied that I had thought of everything. When night fell and Corpus Delicti was enshrouded in darkness, I smuggled Roxanne Doggerel in through the college garden. She was responding to the venture with enthusiasm.

'Are you sure that's *all* you want me to do, Chris?'

'It will be more than enough.'

'Seems small recompense for what you did for me.' She put an arm around my shoulders. 'Why don't I come round every night for a week!'

'That would be gilding the lily, Roxanne.'

When we got to my room, I showed her the costume that had been delivered that morning. She shook with mirth and began to undress at once. I popped into the bedroom to check that all was in readiness. Lying white-faced and naked beneath the sheets, Ferriday was having first night nerves. He hissed at me between chattering teeth.

'What do I *do*, Mountjoy?'

'Take it lying down.'

'Are you certain this is going to work?'

'You'll never look at another copper beech.'

When I had calmed him down, I switched off the light and inched open the door to look at Roxanne. She was absolutely stupendous. Her bronze breastplate gleamed with warlike purpose and her huge breasts bulged over the top in a mood of excess. The tiny skirt gave me my first sight of her magnificent thighs, two tree trunks of wobbling sensuality that made me buzz all over. Armour plates guarded her shins and she wore loose sandals on her broad feet.

Aggressively feminine in her usual donkey jacket and slit skirt, she was now positively overpowering. I longed to change places with Ferriday and surrender willingly to this Queen of Boadiceas.

'Ready?' she bellowed, working herself up for combat.

'Almost!'

I took one last look at her sexual superabundance then I crossed to the window and opened it. Her bellow intensified.

'I take no prisoners!' she warned.

Ferriday panicked. 'Mountjoy, I'm not up to this.'

'You soon will be.' I gave the signal. 'Ready!'

'CHARGE!' yelled Roxanne.

Descending the drainpipe, I heard sounds of passion and invasion as the newly-elected Professor of Poetry at Oxford fleshed herself upon Ferriday and left him for dead.

I felt proud of what I had done. It is not given to everyone to help a friend in such dire need and to make the London Underground a safe place for fur coats to travel on.

When Bernard came into the bedroom next morning, there were chariot marks everywhere.

The Boat Race was held on the Saturday after we went down and I honoured my promise to Emmeline by going along and standing on the boat near the finish. Vast crowds lined the route and the atmosphere built to a peak as the starting time approached. It is the one day of the year when London seems to remember that it has a river and the Thames gets special status. Its dark waters were covered with flotillas of boats and barges.

Davinia had bought a new outfit for the occasion. She had a fur-trimmed gold anorak with a matching hat and black trousers with a thin gold stripe down them. The gold boots kept out the cold wind and shone in the sunshine. She was determined to be noticed.

'Fancy a small bet, Christopher?' she challenged.

'No, thank you.'

'My money would be on Cambridge.'

'They haven't won for eight consecutive years, Davinia.'

'Something tells me this might be their day.'

A mighty roar from further down the river told us that the race was under way and we crowded around a radio to hear the commentary. It was supplemented by the crowd reaction on banks and bridges as the crews sliced their way along the course. Oxford, by the sound of it, had a slight advantage. I could picture Emmeline urging on her eight with orders and exhortations. When the commentator told us that the Oxford boat was now almost a length ahead, I could not resist a dig at my sister.

'What price Cambridge now?'

'There's still some way to go yet,' she said complacently.

'Emmeline will bring them home with their tails up.'

'Emmeline' she sneered. 'The President of the Christopher Mountjoy Fan Club, you mean!'

'I won't have a word said against her!' I warned.

'She's got a surprise coming. So have you.'

We could now see the crews in the distance, dipping their oars in the choppy water and then heaving together with all their might. They must have been a quarter of a mile away when Cambridge put in a spurt and began to overhaul the Oxford boat. I could see Emmeline's head turn in distress to look at the rival crew. She leant forward to call for more from her own eight but they had shot their bolt.

The crews were neck and neck and the noise reached pandemonium level. Cambridge then began to pull away and Davinia smiled.

'I told you Oxford would lose,' she said. 'I said the same to Neil Blythe. Last night.'

'Last night! Davinia, you didn't . . . ?'

'Only once. Or maybe it was twice.' She grinned with satisfaction as the Oxford crew began to fade even more. 'It was certainly twice with Mark Tewson. He's the one sitting behind Neil . . . '

Davinia had got her revenge on me. Madly jealous of my success at Oxford in the play and during the election for the new Professor of Poetry, she was determined to steal any glory that I might get out of the Boat Race. Emmeline was drawing strength from my presence but Davinia was thwarting the cox. On the night before the race, she had drawn strength from at least two of the crew and left them struggling when the pressure was really on.

Cambridge shot past the finishing line to thunderous applause. Limping behind them came the sad, dispirited, beaten Oxford crew. Neil Blythe looked half-dead and Mark Tewson was bent double.

'You really are a cow, Davinia!' I informed her.

'It was rather nice,' she said airily. 'All that pent-up energy.'

'Is *nothing* sacred?'

'Well done, Cambridge!' she shouted through cupped hands.

'You disgust me!' I said.

'Oh go away!'

She pushed me with such force that I lost my balance and fell over the side of the boat into the water. The splash made the dejected Emmeline sit up and take notice. When she saw me surface, she hurled her megaphone aside and dived overboard to help me. She was on me within seconds.

'Stop struggling, Christopher!'

'But I can *swim*!'

'This is no time to be argumentative.'

After suffering the disappointment of losing the race, Emmeline was going to win something. Forcing me on to my back so that I would float, she slipped her hand between my legs to take a firm but gentle grip and towed me towards the furthest bank.

'Emmeline, what are you *doing*?' I gurgled.

'Just go with the tide . . . '

Which is exactly what I did.

Chapter Twelve:
MAY BALLS

Easter that year was marked by a singular occurrence. The entire Mountjoy family went to Communion Service on Easter Day at the Parish Church of St. Saviour's, Hampton Magna. Since none of us had expected to see any of the others, there was a fair amount of surprise and confusion but we eventually came to terms with the phenomenon and shuffled into the family pew.

We sat in descending order of importance – father, mother, Barnaby, Davinia, myself and Hannibal the poodle.

'Is your dear wife not with us, Barnaby?'

'No mother. She is back at the house.'

'Indisposed?'

'Temporarily.'

Barnaby's wife was recovering from another form of communion. Having accepted the wisdom of doing everything in triplicate, she made love to her husband three times every Sunday morning. Religiously. As Barnaby had explained to her, if he forgot the first time – even the second – there would always be the third to think about during the duller stretches of the sermon.

My parents had their first conversation of the year.

'Rather crowded in here,' observed father.

'It's such a small church, Marcus. With us taking up so much room, over half the congregation will have to stand outside.'

'They won't mind that. The rain is not all that heavy.

Besides, when the Mountjoys are in residence, the lesser must bow to the greater. So it is ordained.'

'You have such a gift for words, Marcus.'

'Who is that garden gnome wearing a white nightshirt?'

'That is the vicar in his surplice.'

'Couldn't the Parish afford a larger size in parson?'

The service began. Small in stature, the vicar was big in voice and his Stentorian delivery made it possible for those standing outside between the tombstones to share in our worship. Hymns posed the only real problem. Because the *al fresco* section was operating in a different time zone, they were four bars behind us during the singing and sounded like an echo effect that had been electronically imposed by a mischievous angel fiddling with the knobs.

I could have chosen nicer neighbours. Davinia took every chance she could to punch, elbow or kick me and Hannibal, having threatened to irrigate my trouser leg, tried to leave a more dramatic memento on my shoe. Even in the House of the Lord, Mountjoys remained true to themselves. When the offertory plate came around, father leaned over to the churchwarden.

'Look here, my good fellow . . . '

'Yes, Sir Marcus?'

'Do you take American Express?'

Mother's adherence to her own code of behaviour was equally strict. As she knelt at the altar rails and was confronted by a chalice containing red liquid of an inferior vintage, she looked up at the vicar as if he were an unhelpful waiter.

'Could you bring the wine list, please?'

It was that sort of occasion.

For me, of course, it had a special significance because it took my mind back to the funeral of Great-Aunt Lucy when I had sat in the same church with mother and that pride of elderly gentlemen. Affectionate memories of the dear departed led me on to the provisions of her will. My eighteenth birthday was now within sight and I would soon come into my inheritance.

One hundred thousand pounds and a Visitors Book.

The final hymn interrupted my reverie. As we sang 'Lord Dismiss Us With Thy Blessing', the echo effect outside seemed to accelerate until it overtook us. At the precise moment when the two congregations were actually singing in tune, I heard a lone voice booming out a different hymn altogether and calling for aid for those in peril on the sea.

Nanny Groat was out there, after all.

As we poured out of the church, we made a strange discovery.

'I'm going back to Mountjoy Manor,' announced father.

'So am I, Marcus,' said mother.

'And I,' added Barnaby.

'Me, too,' remarked Davinia.

'Yes,' I admitted.

Not to be left out of it, Hannibal yapped in the affirmative.

Having established a common destination, we all made our own ways there by separate means. I never caught sight of any of them for the rest of the holiday.

Trinity Term at Oxford is a time of extremes. For third and fourth-year undergraduates it means Finals and for everybody else it means fun. Libraries are full of grim-faced strangers, trying to repair the damage in one last desperate crash programme of study and the river is full of punts. Work or wonderland. Oxford gives you the choice. I opted for the latter.

'We don't have any lectures at all this term, Gordy.'

'Why not?'

'Chuck Novis doesn't believe in them. He thinks that practical experience is far more useful than taking lecture notes.'

'So all you do is chop down trees and dig holes?'

'Don't forget the Open Day at the monastery.'

Gordy Hollis had won a Music Scholarship at nearby Hoaryhole College and he had come to Oxford one Saturday to meet his tutor. I was delighted to be able to give him a proper tea this time. His mind was still preoccupied with Carlotta Nashe.

'She does say some very odd things, Christopher.'

'Does she?'

'When I told her about my Music Scholarship, she said she was amazed that you hadn't won an Organ Exhibition.' His face puckered. 'When I explained that you didn't play any instrument, she laughed.'

'Carlotta is a strange girl,' I conceded.

'Strange but unworldly,' said Gordy fondly. 'I'd love to be able to bring her to full fruition as a woman.'

I bit back my rejoinder. We munched cake and talked some more.

'Gordy . . . ' I said over a third cup of tea.

'Yes?'

'Does Rosemary Anne like dancing?'

'Dancing?'

'Two people moving around to music.'

'Yes. She's rather good at it.'

Rosemary Anne was good at everything. It was one of the many reasons that I was so inextricably in love with her. I tried to sound offhand.

'If someone were to invite her to a May Ball at an Oxford college, do you think she'd be at all interested?'

'I *know* she'd be interested!' he asserted.

'You know it for a fact?'

'Yes, Christopher. Why do you ask?'

'Excuse me,' I said.

Showing a turn of speed that Ferriday in his heyday could not have matched, I vanished from the room and raced off to the lodge. The College Porter was his amiable and inquisitive self.

'Where you bloody phoning, Mr Mountjoy?'

'Cheltenham Ladies' College.'

'Ask them to send a Cheltenham Bloody Lady for me!'

'I'm calling a friend.'

'I can be bloody friendly if a lady gives me the bloody chance.'

After feeding the machine with coins and waiting while somebody went to fetch Rosemary Anne, I eventually heard her voice at the end of the line. She was pleased but puzzled to hear from me. It was odd that I should feel so nervous when she and I had twice almost gone to bed together but I did. Filling my lungs, I got my sentence out in one gabble.

'If someone were to invite you to a May Ball at an Oxford college, do you think you'd be at all interested?'

'I'd be absolutely delighted!'

'That's marvellous!'

'What girl wouldn't be thrilled to have such an offer. I'd have to be potty to refuse it.'

'Then you'll come to Corpus Delicti?'

'I'm afraid not, Christopher.'

'But we're having this May Ball,' I stressed. 'It's in May.'

'Sorry.'

'You just said that – '

'That I'd be delighted to be asked. And I was. Last week.'

'Last week?'

'By Simon Vambrace.'

'Simon *who*?' I demanded, loathing him immediately.

'Vambrace. His sister, Diana, is at Cheltenham with me. I met Simon last hols when I stayed with them. He rang me up out of the blue to say he had two tickets for the May Ball at Christ Almighty!'

'Christ Almighty!'

'That's right,' she said, mistaking my exclamation for repetition. 'Simon reckons it's going to be a super affair.'

'Corpus Delicti's Ball will be much better,' I argued. 'We're selling a hundred tickets.'

'Christ Almighty! has printed six hundred.'

'We've hired this terrific pianist from Cowley Workingmen's Club.'

'They've got Syd Lawrence and his Orchestra.'

'Our cabaret features Stromboli the Fire-Eater!'

'They've got Michael Jackson.'

‘We’re offering three choices of sandwich and a non-alcoholic punch!’ I boasted proudly.

‘Christ Almighty! starts with a champagne supper and ends with a champagne breakfast.’

I gave up. We just could not compete. She sensed my disappointment.

‘If you’d asked me first, I’d have accepted like a flash. But Simon beat you to the draw . . . By the way, do you know him?’

‘No, Rosemary Anne, and I’m not sure that I want to.’

‘Simon is President of the Union.’

‘I never go. Prefer the cinema.’

She tried to ease my pain. ‘I’m sure that Carlotta would come with you, if you asked her . . . ’

‘Goodbye,’ I said and put the receiver down.

Gordy was now standing beside me with a shamefaced grin.

‘I meant to tell you about Simon Vambrace.’

‘You let me walk right into that, Gordy! Thank you!’

I stormed back to my room, made another cup of tea and brooded in silence for a long time. When I finally came out of my brown study, Gordy was sitting patiently on the sofa. He had the hopeful look of a spaniel waiting for its master to toss it a scrap of food.

‘Did she say anything about Carlotta?’ he asked.

Friendship alone saved him from certain death.

A term that should have been heaven slowly turned into hell. Instead of luxuriating in the pleasures of Oxford, I spent all my time thinking about Rosemary Anne. To have my invitation turned down was bad enough: to learn that she would be at an adjacent and much more expensive Ball with the President of the Union was like having a hot needle embedded in my brain. My eighteenth birthday fell on the day after the Ball. Had Rosemary Anne been with me, we could have retired to my room at midnight and celebrated my arrival at manhood. It was the most important day of my life so far and she would not be there.

I took my discontent to the Junior Common Room and flicked idly through some magazines. Unwanted company arrived.

'Looking forward to the Ball, Mountjoy?'

It was Ferriday. Bright, bouncy, eager, affable, reformed.

'No!' I growled.

'It's going to be a night of wine and roses!' he announced, beaming down at me. 'Who are you bringing?'

'Myself.'

'No partner?' I shook my head. 'But you could have the pick of any woman in Oxford.'

'I want one from Cheltenham.'

'What?'

'Nothing.' I threw my magazine aside. 'Who are you bringing?'

'Zelda. She's a Karate Instructor from Headington.'

'Karate?'

'I'm into all-action girls at the moment.'

Ferriday had undergone a metamorphosis. A night beneath the Professor of Poetry had opened countless doors to him and he had gone through them in the spirit of adventure. He was smarter, chirpier and altogether more confident.

'They call me P.C.C. Ferriday now.'

'Parochial Church Council?'

'Portnoy's Complaint (Cured). I like it.'

'I was glad to be of some service.'

'Well, I want to be of some service to you now, old chap. There must be somebody you want to bring to the Ball.'

'There isn't.'

'What about that sweet little cox?'

'Emmeline?'

'She had quite a crush on you at the Boat Race.'

'I know,' I recalled. 'I can still feel her hand.'

'What kind of girl would you like, Mountjoy?'

'No kind,' I said with a shrug. 'Right now, I need someone to knock some sense into me. To kick me head-first out of this rotten mood I seem to be in all the time.' I looked up at him. 'Why are you grinning, Ferriday?'

'I don't know,' he said. And his grin broadened.

I had been invited by Sir Joshua Flusher to dine at High Table that evening so that we could discuss plans for the new Mountjoy Annexe. As I headed for the Master's lodgings, I found that Rosemary Anne was still monopolizing my attention and resigned myself to another session of morbid introspection.

Bristol Cream was thrust into my hand as I entered the room.

'Come in, Mountjoy,' welcomed Sir Joshua, flapping about in his gown like a large bird trying to get airborne. 'I'd like you to meet our distinguished guests for the evening. The Vice-Chancellor and his wife – Sir Hamilton and Lady Jaundice.'

Not expecting other guests, I was taken aback to see the portly, greying, middle-aged man with a monocle standing there. When I turned to his wife, my surprise became astonishment. She was gorgeous. Over twenty years separated them and where he was fashionably untidy, she was dressed in a superb full-length gown of black silk.

Lady Jaundice had poise, elegance and a sophisticated charm. Her heart-shaped face featured ruby lips and a pair of striking emerald eyes. Though her body was slim, her breasts were heavy and a generous amount of cleavage was visible down the front of her dress.

My gaze was frankly admiring but she did not return it. All I got was a neùtral and dispassionate stare. Even this was an improvement on what I gained from her husband. The Vice-Chancellor's manner was cold, mocking and judgmental.

'What is your target for this term?' he asked.

'I beg your pardon, Sir Hamilton?'

'We need to shore up our defences. Where do you intend to strike?'

'Nowhere,' I replied with a baffled frown.

'In Michaelmas Term you sabotaged a major theatrical production and set the reputation of OUDS back fifty years,' he accused. 'In Hilary Term you helped to lever a cretinous, no-talent female into the Chair of Poetry and – I am given to understand – you were indirectly involved in Oxford's downfall during the Boat Race.'

'It wasn't quite like that, Vice-Chancellor,' appeased Sir Joshua.

'No,' I agreed. 'It was all unintentional.'

'Unintentional damage is the worst kind!' snarled the visitor, letting his monocle fall from his eye. 'I am watching you, Mountjoy. One more "unintentional" act of folly or destruction and there will be severe repercussions.'

'More sherry anyone?' offered the Master.

I was glad when it was time to go in to dinner.

My reaction to Lady Jaundice was multiplied the length and breadth of the refectory as we entered. Everyone gaped. Chuck Novis, my tutorial triumvirate, stopped chewing his gum and stared at her with the professional eye of a log-roller assessing a particularly troublesome piece of timber.

Before we sat down, grace was read out in Latin by Neil Blythe. The hapless oarsman was so mesmerized by the dark beauty who had just come in that he made a complete mess of the grace. Such an offence by the scholar on duty is punishable and a note duly arrived at the High Table suggesting that Neil should be sconced. When the sconce was ratified, one of the college servants went over to Neil.

'What do you choose, sir?'

'Beer.'

A silver tankard holding two and a half pints of it was soon set in front of him and the whole refectory turned to watch.

'He'll never do it,' said the Master.

Sir Joshua was right. Neil's task was to empty the tankard at one draught and so avoid paying for the beer. If he failed, then he was liable for the bill. He tried hard and shifted about a pint but had to give up. Groans of sympathy rang out. The tankard was now passed to his neighbour who was allowed a free sip before handing it on. For the first time since she had come into the refectory, Lady Jaundice evinced some interest. When the tankard had been through no more than a couple of pairs of hands, she waved to a servant.

'Bring it here, please.'

'Audrey!' protested her husband, turning yellow.

It was unusual for a sconcing stoup to reach the High Table at all and quite unprecedented for it to be summoned by a woman. The whole refectory was hypnotized.

Like a true performer, Lady Jaundice did not rush things. After wiping the rim of the tankard with her handkerchief, she peered in at the liquid and shook it gently around. Then she raised it to her lips and drank, leaving us to feast our eyes on her long white neck and its string of pearls.

'She's done it!' announced Sir Joshua.

'Well done!' I said.

When she held the tankard upside down to prove that it was quite empty, the place erupted. The Vice-Chancellor's wife had just quaffed over a pint of beer in one long go. Instead of acknowledging the applause, she calmly picked up her spoon and made a start on her soup.

The Vice-Chancellor tried to hide his embarrassment beneath another attack on me. 'Be warned, Mountjoy!'

'Yes, Sir Hamilton.'

'I knew your father at Maudlin. Same irresponsible streak.'

'Oh no!' intervened Sir Joshua hastily. 'Sir Marcus has been a generous friend to Corpus Delicti.'

'Sending his son here was an act of revenge not generosity!'

'I must disagree, Vice-Chancellor,' replied Sir Joshua, searching vainly for a Latin tag to cover the situation. 'Since he has been with us, Mr Mountjoy has proved himself – '

'A walking disaster area!'

'No!'

'You're right. A *running* disaster area!'

'Mr Mountjoy has been tipped for a First.'

'In what? Advanced Demolition?'

'That's a bit harsh, Sir Hamilton,' I opined.

He rounded on me viciously. 'I am still pressing for a recount in the election. That freak did not win the Chair of Poetry.'

'No,' I replied. 'W.H. Hauden-Smith lost it. On a technicality. He turned out to be dead.'

'Death enhances a poet!' argued the Vice-Chancellor.

'A NON SEQUITUR, if you don't mind my saying so,' remarked Sir Joshua. He turned to me. 'You see? I did look it up in my dictionary.'

The Vice-Chancellor banged the table to emphasize his point.

'The election should be declared void so that those who voted for Hauden-Smith can transfer their votes to the other candidates and defeat Miss, Mrs, Ms – or whatever she calls herself – Doggerel!'

'*Professor* Doggerel!' I told him.

I stopped short as I realized that I was sitting at a High Table and arguing in blunt terms with one of the most senior men in the university. The explanation was simple. I was jealous of him. I could not bear the thought that he owned, touched, slept with the lovely Lady Jaundice. As I glanced across at her impassive face, I coveted her and let her know it with my eyes. In return, I got a cool stare that was both puzzling and provocative.

Determined to have the last word on the subject, the Vice-Chancellor inserted his monocle then yelled at the top of his voice.

'Nobody in their right mind would vote for Roxanne Doggerel!'

His cry had silenced the refectory. His wife broke that silence.

'I voted for her,' she said proudly.

Her husband collapsed visibly and said no more on the subject.

When the meal was finally over, the Vice-Chancellor

grunted his thanks and hustled his wife away. I went back with the Master for a brandy and some recollection in tranquillity.

Sir Joshua peered at me in consternation.

'I hope you weren't offended by the Vice-Chancellor's comments about your dear father?'

'Don't worry,' I assured him. 'It won't affect the construction of the Mountjoy Annexe.'

'That's very comforting!'

'They're such a peculiar couple, aren't they?' I said, musing on the evening's table talk. 'How long have they been married?'

'About six months. Lady Jaundice is his second wife.'

'What happened to his first wife?'

'She did.'

I took his point. Faced with competition like the current Lady Jaundice, very few women would come out on top. She could have taken a Romeo from a Juliet with not a word spoken.

We chatted until the brandy ran out then I moved to the door.

'If it's not a rude question, Sir Joshua . . . '

'Go ahead and ask it, Mountjoy.'

'Why on earth did you invite such a disagreeable man to dinner?'

'I didn't. He invited himself.'

'Simply to take a crack at me?'

'I don't believe it was his doing at all.'

'What's that?'

'Living in the Ancient World, as I do, one becomes attuned to the nuances of human behaviour. I have seen it all so many times before, Mountjoy. In Livy. In Plutarch. In Herodotus even.'

'Seen what?'

'Deviousness.'

'Could you enlarge on that, Sir Joshua?'

'If you had the time, I could give you a two-hour lecture without notes. As it is, I will reduce it to one telling sentence. The Vice-Chancellor came here this evening because his wife wanted to meet Christopher Mountjoy.'

'But she hardly spoke a word to me all evening!'

'She didn't need to . . . '

I walked out in a complete daze.

After a reflective stroll around the quadrangle, I turned towards my staircase. Rosemary Anne Hollis had been banished from my mind now and it was Lady Jaundice who filled my thoughts. I was still doting on her exquisite neck when I opened the door to my room and switched on the light. Nothing happened. At first I thought the bulb had gone, then I became aware that somebody was in the room.

'Who is it? Who's there?'

I blundered forward and a hand took mine. The next moment, I was hurled bodily through the air to land on my back. When I tried to get up, a naked foot hit me across the back of the neck and made me reel. I struggled up again and expert hands were waiting for me. Using my strength against me, they threw me to the carpet again.

'Who the devil are you?' I gasped.

The small figure of my assailant crossed to open the bedroom door slightly and switched on the light in there. Enough of it spilled out for me to see that I had been attacked by a young, brown-skinned woman who was quite naked. She came and stood menacingly over me. As I tried to rise, she kicked me down. When I grabbed for her foot, she eluded me with ease.

And so it went on. I was repeatedly kicked, punched, chopped, thrown and subdued in a way that somehow brought more pleasure than pain. Though I was aching all over and covered in perspiration, I was also aroused to a degree that had never happened before.

She noticed. Switching her tactics, she suddenly fell across me and began to writhe and twist and roll. The sensation was quite indescribably beautiful. She was massaging me with her whole body and I just lay there in ecstasy. After several minutes of rubbing and kneading me from head to foot, she eased herself off me. Deft fingers touched my belt and zip then my trousers and shorts were removed in one swift pull.

Crouching over me, she used her hands to stroke and excite. Her body moved sensuously to and fro and I was mesmerized. All at once, without warning, she swooped downwards and I was inside her, feeling her stiffen and tremble as she took the full length of the thrust. I stayed on my back in sheer wonderment as she rose and fell and rotated with gathering momentum until she let out a short and intense scream of delight.

Leaning gently forward, she brushed my lips with a kiss of thanks then lifted herself off me. I pleaded for her to stay but she was already clambering into her clothes. Before I could stop her, she had flitted out through the door.

I was still recovering when Ferriday looked in.

'That was Zelda,' he explained. 'I asked her to fit you in as a favour to me. Well, you *did* say you wanted someone to knock some sense into you . . . !'

Chapter Thirteen: NON SEQUITUR

Weeks glided past and the preparation for the May Ball continued in earnest. A marquee was erected in the quadrangle and a wooden floor was laid for dancing. In the college garden, a refreshment tent was set up and filled with trestle tables and folding chairs. Flags and streamers added colour everywhere. There was even bunting on the College Bloody Porter.

Corpus Delicti was letting its back hair down.

Activity was high somewhere else as well.

'I hope the noise hasn't disturbed you, Mr Mountjoy?'

'Noise, Bernard?'

'From Christ Almighty!'

'Ah, you mean that thunderstorm last night?'

'No, sir,' he explained making my bed with his usual attention to detail. 'I was speaking of the college next door. Someone called Barbra Streisand is to blame for all the commotion. I do not know this female person.'

'Barbra Streisand is appearing in their cabaret with Michael Jackson. They're both world-famous singers.'

'Singers, is it, sir?' he said with a sniff.

'The best.'

'They will never improve on Vera Lynn!'

'Coming back to the noise . . . '

'Because these singers is flying in from America in a private jet, they are having to build a runway in Tom Quad. That is what the noise is all about.'

'It's only reasonable, Bernard.'

'I call it a downright liberty, sir.'

'You can't expect superstars to drop in by parachute.'

'There is other means of transport, sir,' he insisted. 'Look at Stromboli the Fire-Eater. He will be arriving on the six-thirty bus from Abingdon where he works by day as a a Male Nurse.' Bernard took out his box of matches and shook them. 'Stromboli has done me the honour of asking me if I will light for him.'

'You can do some more ignition for me as well,' I told him.

'Yes, I see you've bagged the letters up.'

'They've been coming in hundreds.'

'More filth? More suggestions about bodily contact?'

'They're all from women offering to go to the Ball with me.'

'I will burn them, sir. Better still, I'll get Stromboli to burn them as part of his act.' He subjected me to a shrewd stare. 'Are we going to the Ball, then, sir?'

'Probably.'

'Alone?'

'That's in the air at the moment. Why?'

'I wanted to discuss retirement, sir.'

'But you're far too young to retire!' I urged.

'Retirement in this room, sir.'

'I'm sorry, Bernard. Much as I like you, I don't really think the place is big enough for two of us.'

'Retirement during the *Ball*!' he clarified. 'Some young gentlemen – not mine, of course – like to retire with their young ladies to . . . to . . . to the privacy of their rooms to . . . to . . . to "rest". I don't hold with it myself, Mr Mountjoy.'

'With rest?'

'With what comes before it, sir.'

'Say no more. I would do nothing in this room to upset you.'

'I am pleased to hear that, Mr Mountjoy. I would hate to come into your bedroom on the morning after the Ball and find . . . things.'

'What sort of things, Bernard?'

'Objects, sir.'

'Of what nature?'

'*Used.*'

'Cigarette ends?'

'Put it this way, sir,' he said pointedly. 'I would like to walk into a young gentleman's bedroom – not into a balloon factory.

On this warning note, he shook his box of matches and withdrew.

When the term had started the only person I wanted to take to the Ball was Rosemary Anne Hollis. She had been replaced as a target. My sights were now set on Lady Jaundice, the beautiful but inaccessible wife of the Vice-Chancellor. Desire for her and anger for him spurred me on. It was an impossible dream, maybe, but one that gave me untold pleasure and fired me with immense determination.

Christopher Mountjoy with Audrey Jaundice. The unsuitable in pursuit of the unattainable. But it was worth a try.

'Lady Jaundice?'

'Yes?' Her voice was crisp and unwelcoming over the telephone.

'This is Christopher Mountjoy . . .'

'What do you want?'

'I'm terribly sorry to bother you . . .'

'Then don't.'

She slammed the receiver down. Back to the drawing board.

Having found out where she lived, I lurked outside her house in the hopes of a chance meeting. Three long hours of standing beneath a tree eventually brought their reward. Lady Jaundice came out of the house in a smart cream suit and went into the garage. I left my hiding place and darted across the road. As the Porsche nosed its way down the drive, I timed my move to give the impression that I was strolling casually by.

'Hello there!' I greeted, miming surprise.

'What are you doing here?' she asked frostily through the open window. 'Were you waiting for me?'

'I just happened to be passing, Lady Jaundice.'

'In a cul-de-sac?'

'Lovely car!' I noted, patting the bonnet. 'Somehow, I didn't see the Vice-Chancellor as a Porsche man.'

'He has a Rover: this is mine.'

'It suits you, Lady Jaundice. Sleek, smooth and sporty.'

'Stop bothering me, please.'

'I wanted a word with you, that's all.'

'I am in a hurry, Mr Mountjoy. I have to get to the station.'

'Can I give you a lift?' I offered involuntarily, overlooking the fact that I had no transport.

'No,' she retorted. 'I don't think I'd like to be taken for a ride by you.' She put the car into gear. 'Out of my way.'

'I don't suppose you'd have a chat with me some time over a cup of tea, would you?'

The Porsche roared its impatience then shot past me and sped up the road. Tea was obviously not her beverage. Maybe I should have offered her a two-and-a-half pint silver tankard of beer.

I tried notes and sent small presents but they produced no response at all. My telephone calls never lasted more than two seconds. She was playing hard to get with a vengeance. As my failures multiplied, I began to lose heart.

It was Sir Joshua Flusher who gave me a ray of hope. On the morning of the Ball, I met him in the lodge brandishing a large placard in his hand.

'Ah, Mountjoy! The very man!'

'Good morning, Sir Joshua.'

'I have some excellent news for you.'

'Oh?'

'One moment . . . '

He broke off while he pinned his placard on the noticeboard and stood back to admire the Latin phrase that was printed on it in bold black letters.

'This excellent news, Sir Joshua . . . '

'What? Ah yes. They have refused.'

'Who have?'

'The Vice-Chancellor and his wife.'

My interest quickened. 'Refused what?'

'The invitation to the Corpus Delicti Ball.'

'You asked them *here*?'

'Only out of courtesy. He is the Vice-Chancellor, after all. Lady Jaundice was keen to accept our invitation but she was overruled by her husband. They will be going next door instead.'

'To Christ Almighty!?'

'It seems that their Ball is slightly more lavish than ours. Their cabaret will now include an American artiste called Frank Sinatra and they have retained the services of the Band of Coldstream Guards to play at half-time.'

'But Lady Jaundice wanted to come here, you say?'

'Oh yes. When I spoke with her on the telephone, she became almost excited at the prospect. Then the Vice-Chancellor came on the line . . . ' He beamed at me. 'I knew that you'd be relieved at the news.'

'Relieved?'

'That you won't have to put up with his appalling behaviour again. The Vice-Chancellor was inexcusably rude about your father.'

'Oh, don't worry,' I promised. 'I haven't excused him.'

'You were asking me about Lady Jaundice . . . '

'Yes?'

'It transpires that she worked in publishing. They met in connection with his one and only book. She handled him throughout and they were drawn together.'

'What happened to the book?'

'It was remaindered,' he said with candid satisfaction.

I had the feeling that their marriage had met the same fate.

'Thank you for all that you've told me, Sir Joshua.'

'Not at all.' He indicated his placard. 'By the way, let me direct your attention to this general warning I have put up for any of our undergraduates who are coming to the Ball tonight. I do want them to behave as gentlemen.'

I read the words aloud. 'FALLERE CREDENTEM NON EST OPEROSA PUELLAM GLORIA.'

'Give me a rough translation,' he ordered.

'Er . . . "Don't fail to take your credentials when you pull Gloria to the opera . . ." '

'Perhaps it is just as well that you are reading FTI. My own rendering would be: "To deceive a trusting girl is not a glorious or arduous achievement." You see its relevance?'

'Of course.'

'Good, good! I hope it will act as a communal chastity belt.'

Without stopping to wonder how many of the undergraduates would be able to translate the words, he padded back across the quadrangle to the Ancient World. I studied the Latin again. With a slight shift of perspective, it was less a warning than a promise – 'It's there for the taking, chaps! Go and get it!'

The College Porter shook his bunting at me.

'More bloody mail for you, Mr Mountjoy.'

'Is there?'

'Second bloody post.'

'I'll take it up with me now.'

'Your bloody pigeon-hole will need bloody Vaseline on it if your bloody mailbag gets any bloody bigger!'

I took the armful of correspondence up to my room for preliminary sorting, knowing that most of the letters would be offers to accompany me to the Ball. It was paradoxical. Because I had dozens of young women at my beck and call in Oxford, I chose none of them: because there was one who ignored me and resisted my charms, I simply had to conquer her.

One package was quite different from the general run of my mail. When I saw the name of the London solicitors on the address label, I knew what it must be and tore off the brown paper to reveal a large, embossed, leatherbound Visitors Book. It was part of my inheritance from Great-

Aunt Lucy and she expressed the wish – posthumously and in her miniscule handwriting – that I would only permit signatures of those truly worthy to be included.

That night I would come to appreciate what she meant.

A covering letter from the solicitor explained that a cheque for one hundred thousand pounds would be deposited with my bank on Monday morning but that the Visitors Book was being sent so that I could have it – as laid down in the will – on my eighteenth birthday.

I set the book down on my desk and resolved that nobody would sign it until after midnight. Then I turned my mind to the major problem of how I could get to Audrey Jaundice at the Christ Almighty! Ball. It seemed like an impossible mission until I noticed something on my desk. It was the loose-leaf folder in which I kept all my notes on my work.

Forestry. Theology. Industrial Archeology.

My studies might have some practical use after all.

By early evening the first dinner jackets were appearing in the quadrangle to catch the setting sun. There was frantic activity among the catering staff and members of the committee which had organized the Ball were charging around all over the place. The disc jockey tried out his equipment and the College Porter did a solo waltz on the dance floor. Things were starting.

Ferriday called on me in a double-breasted dinner jacket.

'Aren't you changed yet, Mountjoy?'

'There's plenty of time. You look very dashing.'

'I'm just off to pick Zelda up,' he said with a knowing smirk. 'She was very impressed with you, old chap. Don't be surprised if you get a tap on the shoulder during the Ladies' Excuse Me.'

'As long as it's only a tap on the shoulder!' I noted. 'That girl is a real fireball, Ferriday. How ever did you get up enough courage to ask her out?'

'I didn't. She asked me. I went along to her Karate Class one evening and she just threw herself at me.' He adjusted his red cummerbund. 'Oh, I've just seen the cabaret arrive.'

'Stromboli?'

'That's what it said on the suitcases he was carrying. Funny little man with big hands. He looked more like a Male Nurse than a Fire-Eater.'

'You can do a lot with make-up,' I argued.

'I must be off. Zelda hates to be kept waiting.' He paused in the doorway. 'I know one thing, Mountjoy. We should be grateful we're not going to the Christ Almighty! Ball.'

'Why?'

'Because they've locked the gates and put armed guards on them. And they've got hundreds of security guards inside. Christ Almighty himself wouldn't get in there tonight.'

He breezed out and left me to digest the information. I waited for another hour before I put my plan into action. When the Corpus Delicti Ball was well-established, I slipped down the backstairs and sneaked out of the college. Thanks to Chuck Novis, I had an intricate knowledge of the trees in the Meadows and I knew that there was an oak that grew close to Christ Almighty! Its branches overhung the Master's Garden and I was able to lower myself on to the lawn with no real trouble.

Forestry had got me in. Theology now came to my aid.

'Good evening, Father.'

'Good evening, my son,' I replied with an unctuous smile.

'Have you got lost?' asked the security man.

'Yes. Could you direct me to the main marquee?'

He gave me precise instructions and I moved off. I had borrowed a cassock, a dog collar and a hat from a friend at Pusey Chapel and the disguise had been good enough to fool a professional. I was encouraged.

The Ball was at its height. Music blared, feet danced, champagne flowed, voices screeched and there was an air of sophisticated hysteria to the whole proceedings. As Christopher Mountjoy, I would have been recognized at once but as a harmless deacon I could wander at will.

I saw her at once when I reached the main marquee.

Wearing a stunning and revealing ball gown in red satin, Lady Jaundice was circling the dance floor with her husband. He looked ungainly and absurd but she was the picture of elegance and grace. Instead of marring the picture, the bored look on her face only seemed to enhance it.

I was still goggling at her when someone bumped into me.

'Oh, I'm sorry, Father,' said a man's voice.

'My fault,' I piped, keeping my head down.

'Come on, Simon. We don't want to miss this dance.'

'Righto!'

It was Rosemary Anne with a tall, beaky young man in a lightweight dinner jacket. Simon Vambrace, the President of the Union. My envy stirred but it was quickly subdued beneath my guilt. Rosemary Anne looked as glorious as ever in a low-cut green ball gown. If I loved her – as I knew I did – how could I lust after the Vice-Chancellor's wife?

All too easily. It was to be the story of my life.

Pure love set against physical need. Romance wrestling with reality. Innocence at odds with experience. Pedestal versus bed.

When the dance was over, I followed my quarry from a safe distance. Although she was the centre of an admiring circle, the lovely Audrey was as disengaged as ever. After only six months of marriage, she was decidedly jaundiced.

I skulked beneath a canopy and tried to work out how I could make contact with her. Contact of another kind then threatened.

'I say! Hello!'

'What . . . ?' I turned around.

'How are you?'

'Christ Almighty!' I said under my breath.

It was the College Chaplain, spotting a fellow clergyman and bearing down on me as if I was the only other white man in a remote part of Africa. Fear set in as I saw his round, rubicund face smiling at me with Christian fellowship and I took to my heels at once. He was not easily shaken off. Even as I rounded a corner and struck out towards another marquee, I could hear his voice getting closer.

Quite how long we played Chase-me-Charlie I do not know but it seemed an age before I was able to return to Lady Jaundice. I was in luck. She was sitting alone in a small area roped off for VIP's. The sight of her body deconsecrated me on the spot. Her face still had the pained look of the publisher scanning the royalty statements for the Vice-Chancellor's unsaleable book.

I sidled up behind her and got within six feet.

'Stop right there,' she said smoothly.

'What?'

'That's far enough, Mr Mountjoy.'

'How did you know it was me?'

'I could sense it.'

'Listen,' I hissed. 'I must speak with you.'

'Go away!'

'Alone!'

'Go away now!' she insisted.

'If I could just have a few minutes of your – '

'Goodbye, Mr Mountjoy!'

Without sparing me a glance, she got up and sailed off to join her husband at the bar. It had been a signal rejection and yet it only served to increase my desire for her. Beneath my sacred attire, a small furnace was being stoked.

The Chaplain reappeared with two security men.

'There he is!' he yelled, pointing at me.

'Excuse me, sir . . . '

'Could we have a word, sir . . . ?'

'No!' I said.

Hoisting my skirt, I made a rapid and undignified exit. With the three of them in hot pursuit, I dodged and weaved through the crowd and made my way to the nearest building. Even as I dived up the first staircase, I knew that I had been seen. My disguise was now a liability.

When I reached the first landing, I tore off my clerical garb and hurled it into a room. Straightening my bow tie and trying to affect a debonair manner, I descended the stairs in my dinner jacket. The security men met me halfway up.

'Did you see a priest up here, sir?' one asked.

'Yes,' I said. 'He just pushed past me and raced upstairs.'

'That's him!'

As they went up, I went down, shielding my face from the Chaplain who was waiting outside. With my camouflage gone, I was now forced to stay in the shadows and stalk my game from a distance.

Audrey Jaundice was not enjoying the Ball. I saw her refuse to dance time after time and she sat unmoved during the cabaret. With midnight approaching, she stood up and spoke to her husband. From her gestures, I gathered that she was complaining about a headache. She turned and headed towards the main building.

This was my chance. She was going to the retiring room set aside for the Vice-Chancellor. Keeping out of the light, I skirted the quadrangle and watched her go up a staircase on the far side. It took me some while to reach the same point myself so I had no idea which room she had entered.

The first door confronted me. It was no time for a timid knock. Grabbing the handle, I flung the door open to show her my strength of purpose.

'Oh shit!'

'If you're the Vice Squad, mother will kill me!'

I am not sure which of the two young men was the more shocked. They pulled apart violently in a way that could have left permanent damage and reached for their clothes.

'Sorry!' I mumbled and went straight out.

At the top of the next flight of stairs was a much more imposing oak door. This had to be the room reserved for the Vice-Chancellor. Again, I opted for a dramatic entrance and pushed the door so hard that I broke the bolt on the other side.

A small, balding, middle-aged man in underwear was kneeling down and blowing furiously into a life-size plastic doll. He had almost got her up to her full potential when I burst in.

'Did my wife send you!' he cried.

'No.'

'Don't tell her, please! I'll pay you twice what she does!'

In his anguish at being discovered, he let go of the nozzle and his companion gave a long and very unladylike wheeze before ending up in a little heap on the carpet.

'My lips are sealed!' I promised him and ran out.

Then I saw my two security men coming up the stairs after me. Barging back into the room, I parted the loved ones yet again after only a few puffs. I threw up the window, trusted to luck, and jumped. Springy turf gave me a soft landing but I had not escaped.

'That's him, lads!' yelled one of the security men at the window.

'Get him!' urged his sidekick.

Their colleagues seemed to be coming at me from all directions. Now in a blind panic, I ran wildly towards the main marquee where the dancing had been resumed under dimmed lights. Hurling myself on to the stage, I ran helter skelter through the orchestra and turned a gentle waltz into a Dashing White Sergeant. I was lucky to dodge the cymbal that was thrown and I dread to think what might have happened to me if that trombone had been on target.

Everyone now joined in. Chase the Intruder was the name of the game and it seemed to give them enormous fun. Hundreds of them were hounding me as I headed for the Master's Garden and there was no way that I could outrun them. Fortune then smiled on me.

When I saw a narrow pit that had been roped off, I recognized it at once for what it was and swung towards it. Diving into it like a rabbit into a burrow, I grabbed the thick cable in both hands and pulled with all my might.

There was a loud bang as the electricity cut off. Darkness fell at once. Chase the Intruder became Blind Man's Buff. Squeals and giggles suggested that other games were being tried out as well. My initiative below ground had saved me in the nick of time.

Industrial Archeology had at last justified itself.

* * *

Pandemonium continued long enough for me to find the Master's Garden and use my arborial exit. Dirty and dishevelled, I ran to Corpus Delicti and entered through the rear door. The revellers were far too busy enjoying themselves to notice a lone figure creeping past in the shadows. When I got to my staircase, I went up it in leaps and bounds before lunging through my door.

Peace at last. Not even daring to think what repercussions there would be after my visit to Christ Almighty!, I staggered towards the bedroom. I was exhausted and simply wanted to flop down and sleep.

As I blundered into the darkened bedroom, a sultry voice spoke.

'What kept you?'

'Lady Jaundice!'

'This is an occasion when you might call me "Audrey".'

Formality had been cast aside. But for a satin robe, this gorgeous creature was lying naked on my bed. A Rokeby Venus with a lascivious appetite. Womanhood in all its promise and bounty. The full breasts hung like ripe fruit that waited to be picked and her slim body had the sheen of desire on it. She pulled at a grip and soft hair cascaded around her shoulders.

My fatigue vanished and red blood coursed through my veins. The first kiss took me on a magical mystery tour that had me pounding for more. With languid sensuality, she undressed me completely then pulled me to her.

'I thought you didn't want me!' I gasped between kisses.

'Rejection is good for a man.' Her hand closed on me in a grip that brought new rapture. 'It makes him try harder.'

'I wanted you *so* much!' I confessed.

'I know. I can read you like a book.'

The erstwhile publisher used her tongue to copy-edit my whole body. Her expert fingers went through my proofs with tantalizing thoroughness until I was bursting for release. Her whispered voice made corrections in my margin and kept me on the right line. When her thighs suddenly parted and I made contact with a warm haven of wonder, I knew that she had decided on a very large print run.

We let the presses run for minute after miraculous minute and then we celebrated publication with a long, loud cry of mutual joy.

Great Aunt Lucy had come out in hardback.

'Christopher?' she sighed in pure contentment.

'Yes?'

'You have got a bestseller!'

As I lay panting on the bed, she eased herself up and tripped off into the other room to write something in my Visitors Book. At last I realized what that gift was for and I was thrilled that hers would be the first name to grace its pages.

'Move over,' she said, getting back on the bed. 'I'm ready again.'

'For what?'

'A second edition.'

It sold even more copies than the first.

Afterwards, she faded into the night like a spirit and I was left to catch my breath and reflect on what had happened. Audrey had found me a young novice and left me a grown man. She had taken something from me but given far more in return. She had ensured my early departure from Oxford but she was sending me on to higher branches of learning.

It was my eighteenth birthday and I had truly come of age.

I went next door to look at my Visitors Book. She had signed her name with a flourish and added two words by way of comment.

'Follow that!'

At last I had my own translation for the family motto.

NON SEQUITUR.

Follow that!

In the next volume of my Memoirs, I will . . .